# MURDER ON THE WIND

*Book Two In The*
*O'Toole/Starker*
*Murder Mystery Series*

## G. A. Cockerham

This is a work of fiction. Names, characters, businesses, places, events and incidents are either the products of the author's imagination or used in a fictitious manner. Any resemblance to actual persons, living or dead, or actual events is purely coincidental.

ISBN-13: 9780989240840

# ACKNOWLEDGEMENTS

I give thanks to my husband, Bruce, whose technical knowledge maintains reality within my stories, and whose constant support and encouragement helps me through the pauses in my creativity.

Bruce is a retired police captain with thirty years' experience in law enforcement. He has worked in patrol, traffic, detectives, SWAT, and administration and also worked as an academy instructor. He trained with the FBI as a counter sniper, and is a graduate of both the California Command College and the FBI National Academy. He holds a BA from Whitworth University and an MDiv from San Francisco Theological Seminary. He currently serves with the Curry County Sheriff's Office as a civil-enforcement deputy.

# Table of Contents

# CHAPTER 1

Patty knew this was more than a routine welfare check on a missing person when she and her partner, Rick, drove up to the small, secluded house about a half mile off the Chetco River North Bank Road, running east from Highway 101. Rick turned to Patty as they rocked and rolled on the narrow road, barely useable due to deep potholes. "Just our luck to have no patrol officers available to take this call."

Patty smiled. "We're lucky it's July and the ground is dry. Three months ago this would have been a muddy mess."

Rick called in the location before they stepped out of the car and onto a path that meandered through a group of fir trees before opening into a large open area with a small house. Stepping up to the porch, she observed that the door appeared to have been opened with force, breaking the lock. She turned to Rick and then pointed to the doorknob lying a few feet away on the bare living room floor. The air was thick with flies and the smell was something she'd never get used to. With guns drawn, Patty and Rick walked through the door into the large open room that served as a combined kitchen/living room. Finding no threat, the two detectives continued down a hall toward the other end of the house. It was a typical hallway, with doors on both sides and a bathroom at the end.

Patty gestured for Rick to go left. Clearing the first two rooms, they walked to the end of the hall and entered through a final doorway. It was evident by the room's size and private bath that it was the master. Given the strong stench and the sight of maggots, it was also clear that the body lying face up on the bed, a fully-clothed woman, had been dead for some time. Nothing in the room seemed amiss except for a glass ashtray on the floor.

Patty called it in while Rick went out to the car to get the camera, gloves, and crime-scene booties for each of them. "This is O'Toole, and we've got a dead body at 36350 Winston Way. We need a couple of officers and Deputy Coroner Ted Kindle."

Rick returned with the camera and Patty filled him in. "Brad responded to my call and should be here in about ten minutes. Kindle just finished up in Pistol River and is on his way. That means we've got at least another half hour before he arrives, and it could be close to twice that depending on the number of roadwork delays."

"Work on that stretch of road was going on when I moved here three years ago," Rick said. "Has it always been a problem?"

"As long as I can remember," Patty said. "The land is pretty unstable around the Hooskenaden area, and the ground movement causes an ongoing need for repaving."

Rick removed the camera from its case. "I guess for most people the view from here to Gold Beach justifies the delays."

Patty smiled. "Yeah, it's hard to complain when you're looking out at those giant sea stacks and beautiful coastline."

Rick started toward the front door and then paused. "Has Curry County always had a deputy coroner?"

Patty nodded. "Yeah, as a specially trained and certified sheriff's deputy, he's the only one who can pronounce someone dead at the scene. Curry County's just too sparsely populated to have our own medical examiner. That's why Curry and about five other southern Oregon counties use Dr. Miller out of Medford."

Rick nodded as he walked toward the side of the house. "I'll start outside and work my way in. How wide a perimeter do you want?"

Patty looked at the landscape around the house. "Let's make it twenty-five yards in all directions. I'll take a closer look in the bedroom. I'm guessing the ashtray we saw on the floor may turn out to be the murder weapon."

A couple of Brookings PD cars pulled up out front and Patty walked out to meet officers Burt Bradley, a seven-year veteran of Brookings PD, and a new Brookings officer, Peter Chekowsky. "Hey Brad," she said, then turned to Chekowsky. "Pete."

"Hi Patty," Brad said. "We were pulled off a burglary report to come here. What have you got?"

"We've got a dead female inside. Judging by the appearance of the blood around her head, Ted may find evidence of a fatal blow. We need to have the area taped around the perimeter of the house about twenty-five yards in all directions. I also need one of you to start a log for the crime scene. Rick and I are the only ones thus far to enter the area. Ted Kindle is coming from Pistol River. Call dispatch if you want and request a reserve to come out and take care of the CS log once you've started it. We want a minimum number of people walking into our crime scene."

"Will do." Brad said as he and Chekowsky walked back to their cars for the CS tape and log sheet.

"Why do the detectives call you Brad instead of Burt?" Chekowsky asked.

"Well," Officer Bradley laughed, "when I first came to this agency there was another officer named Burt. So, to keep us straight, Patty just started calling me Brad. Detective Starker picked up the name from Patty."

Chekowsky nodded and got into his car.

When Rick finished taking photos and video outside, he slipped on a pair of gloves and booties before entering the house and joining Patty, who'd already covered her hands and shoes.

Patty pointed to the kitchen. "There's a purse on the counter. You can take photos while I search for ID."

Rick took a couple of pictures of the purse and its location and then a few more of the wallet as Patty pulled it from the purse and opened it, showing a driver's license for Lola Martin. Looking at the photo she said, "It's hard to compare the photo to the deceased but it looks enough like her that I believe this is her ID." Patty then pulled the portable radio off her belt, paused a moment before putting it back, and took out her cell phone. "I'm going to check in with the LT, and I'm thinking it's best to keep this off of the radio. I think the LT's going to suggest we ask OSP to send out a crime-scene tech since the state has a lot more resources than we have."

Rick started down the hall. "I'll take photos of the victim and ashtray."

Patty dialed the lieutenant's number and got through on the second ring. "This is O'Toole, LT. Rick and I are at the house of the woman who missed the last two days of work at Fred Meyer. She's deceased, and it appears she's probably been dead for two days or more. Ted Kindle's on his way. I'll wait to call the ME until after OSP lets us know if they're going to handle the CS processing. There are no obvious signs of death. However, she's fully clothed and the only blood we see appears to have come from the back of her head. Kindle will turn her over and we'll be in a better position to guess whether if there's a blow to her head, it was enough to kill her."

There was a brief pause on the line, which was normal when talking to the lieutenant. He had moved up in the ranks quickly. This was, in part, due to his keen ability to find clues others missed in working crimes, and to his practice of thinking before speaking, resulting in his generally being right. "Okay, O'Toole. You and Rick stay on this. Contact OSP and let me know who you get. I'll be interested in knowing, too, what Dr. Miller determines as cause of death."

"Will do," Patty said before ending the call and catching up with Rick. "Find anything unusual?"

Rick lowered the camera. "Not really, but for a woman she seems to have few personal items and, it appears, no pictures. I wonder how long she's lived here?"

Patty agreed. "It is pretty empty in here. We'll know more about any family and friends when we talk with her supervisor, who may have to identify the body. She's the one who called in and asked us to check on the deceased due to her missing work, and she might know if this woman had family. I'll never get used to asking relatives to identify the body of someone they loved."

"Yeah," Rick said. "It got a lot harder for me after having to identify my own wife and child. There are no words to explain."

"I'm sure there aren't," Patty said while thinking of Rick's losses. He'd come a long way since Claire and Skylar were murdered, but it was clear that he wasn't the same person. The loss had changed him.

While Rick continued taking photos of several individual items and took videos panning the rooms, Patty stepped out the front door. Standing on the small porch, she put in a call to OSP and had to leave a message. Her next call was to Fred Meyer. After Patty listened to the automated choice of departments, a receptionist answered the call. "Fred Meyer. This is Teresa. May I help you?"

"This is Detective O'Toole with the Brookings Police Department. I need to speak with Karen Gains."

"Please hold on, Detective."

About thirty seconds passed before Patty heard someone on the line. "This is Karen Gains."

"Ms. Gains, this is Detective O'Toole with the Brookings Police Department. You spoke this morning with one of the officers about your employee, Lola Martin."

"Yes, Detective. Lola's missed two days of work without calling in and she hasn't responded to my voicemail messages. Did someone check on her?" she quietly asked.

Patty continued. "We did, and I'm sorry to tell you that Ms. Martin is deceased."

Patty heard a gasp on the other end of the phone, then "Oh my God! Do you know how she died?"

Patty paused before responding. "We're working on that now. My partner, Detective Starker, and I would like to meet and talk with you tomorrow afternoon. Where can you meet us at one?"

"I'll be here, Detective. Just ask for me at the service desk up front and someone will call me."

"We'll do that, Ms. Gains. Can you give me the names of any employees who knew Ms. Martin other than to work with her? Did she have friends who work for Fred Meyer?"

"Well," Ms. Gains said. "Lola didn't have many friends that I know of, but there is one employee who frequently took his break with Lola."

Patty waited, and hearing nothing more, asked, "And the name of this employee?"

"Well, we're not supposed to give out names of employees, Detective. You know how it is."

"I know that this is the investigation of a death, and you wouldn't want to interfere with our investigation by withholding information that may be helpful, Ms. Gains. Would you?"

The supervisor quickly responded. "His name is Ben Brown."

"Thank you, Ms. Gains. Do you happen to know if Mr. Brown is working tomorrow?"

"Well, yes he is," she responded.

"That's good," Patty said. "Please let Mr. Brown know that we'll want to talk with him between two and three o'clock, and that we'll expect to meet with him at Fred Meyer unless he calls the police station and gives an alternate meeting place."

"Okay, Detective. I'll let him know."

"Thank you, Ms. Gains," Patty said. "We'll see you tomorrow at one."

Patty looked up to see Deputy Kindle pulling up. After slipping on his gloves he checked in with the officer keeping the CS log and walked under the yellow tape Officer Bradley had run along the path to the front porch where Patty was standing.

"Hey Ted," she greeted as he reached over to put on his booties. "How's it going?"

"Not bad," he said as he looked across the room. "What have we got?"

Patty filled Ted in on the call and what she and Rick had done thus far. Then pointing down the hall. "The deceased is on a bed in the last bedroom on your left. You'll want to take a look at the large glass ashtray on the floor. It's the only thing we've found in the house that could have been used if you find a blow to the back of her head."

"I'll look at it after I see the body," Ted said as Patty walked ahead of him into the master bedroom. Rick followed the two with his camera.

Ted walked around the foot of the bed and while standing next to it took a moment to first scan the woman's body. "I don't see any obvious clues of how she died." He noted the large, bloody area on the sheet below where the woman's head lay and asked Rick, "You've got full photos?" When Rick nodded yes, Ted turned to Patty. "I don't see anything on her face or the front of her neck that would have caused the bleeding, so I'm going to turn her on her side." Taking hold of the arm closest to him and placing his other arm under the woman's back, he slowly turned her over and away from him. The woman's hair was caked with dried blood, and Ted found what he was looking for when he carefully separated some of the hair. "There's a large gash on the back of her skull. You need to get a few shots of this, Rick."

Rick stood next to Ted and took several photos of the gash as well as the bedsheet.

"Does it look bad enough to have killed her?" Patty asked.

Ted nodded. "Bad enough," he said, and then looked around the room. "Judging by the lack of any blood spatters against the wall, I'd say she wasn't hit while in bed."

Rick pointed to where the ashtray lay. "There appear to be some dark smears of something on the floor between the ashtray and the corner table. She could have been hit there and then placed on the bed."

Patty knelt down and looked more closely at the smears on the floor. "It does look like someone tried to clean up the floor here. It's curious that he'd take the time to both place her on the bed and clean up."

"You think she was hit by someone who knew her?" Rick asked. "Someone who cared about making her comfortable?"

"That's a possibility," Patty said. "Or it could have been a stranger who walked in, startled her, and hit her out of panic. Could be he felt some remorse." Then looking up at Ted, she said, "Would the blow to her head have caused a large amount of blood to flow out quickly?"

"A gash this bad would certainly have produced a lot of blood. You'll know more after the ME examines her. And since it's clear this isn't an accident, I'd recommend that she be examined soon. There may be a killer out there searching for his next victim."

Ted walked to where the ashtray lay and turned it over. "Get a picture of this, Rick. It looks like a few strands of hair are stuck in the blood on the side of the ashtray. This was used to hit someone, and I expect it was our victim."

Rick took a few photos of the ashtray before they all walked back to the front of the house, where Ted turned to Patty. "You'll need a box to transport that ashtray back to the evidence room."

"I'm going to leave it for OSP. They have a more sophisticated system than we do and will probably want to take possession of it from here."

Ted agreed. "The fewer people on the chain of evidence the better. I'll hold off calling the funeral director until after OSP has viewed the scene. Are you and Rick going to wait for their CS tech?"

"No, we're going to head back to the office, and there's probably no reason for you to stay. Brad and Chekowsky will keep the scene secure. I'll let you know what OSP decides to do with the body. Thanks for coming out, and tell the sheriff thanks, too."

Ted stood on the front porch as he turned back to Patty. "No problem. I had just finished up in Pistol River working on a burglary that was reported yesterday."

Patty, Rick, and Ted ducked under the CS tape and then Rick and Ted headed toward their respective cars. "Thanks again," Patty said to Ted as he walked away. She then walked over to where Brad was standing. "Rick and I have done all we can here. A CS tech from OSP is on the way. The tech will want to see the body before it's moved and you'll need to make sure that happens. You'll want to post notices on the door and on several trees around the perimeter."

Brad smiled. "Already got most of them up, and we've got you, Rick, and Ted logged out of the CS log."

"Thanks," Patty said with a smile. "Good to see you're a step ahead of me."

Patty's cell phone rang as she walked toward the car where Rick was putting away his camera.

"O'Toole here," she answered.

"Well, hello O'Toole. This is your mother. How's your day going?"

Patty smiled. "This must mean that you and Bill are back in the states. I'm looking forward to hearing all about your cruise. Are you home?"

"Not quite. We flew from Heathrow into New York, where we now have a six-hour layover before boarding our plane to Portland. We'll spend the night in Portland before driving home so that we have a few hours to adjust to the time change."

"Wow, Mom. That's a lot of travel time. How long was the flight from Heathrow?"

"Oh, that was another eight hours."

"I'm not sure the travel time would be worth the trip for me, Mom. I hope you had a fabulous time."

"It was a great trip, Patty, and Bill bumped us both up to first class, which was an experience in itself. It's the first time I've flown where we each had our own little pod to sit or sleep in. It was really quite comfortable, and Delta's food is great!"

"Seems it was a good trip, Mom, and I look forward to hearing all about it. Why don't you and Bill join Becky and me at our place Sunday? That will give you both time to unwind. I'll ask Rick and Barbara over too."

"That'll be super, Patty. Ta-ta for now, as the Brits say."

"Hope your flight goes well, Mom. Call me when you get to Portland."

"Okay dear. Love you. Bye-bye."

"Bye Mom. Love you too."

Rick couldn't help but overhear Patty's side of the conversation. "Sounds like your mom and Bill had a good trip."

"Yeah, seems they did, even if it took them three days to get to England."

Rick gasped. "Three days! Did they swim across the Atlantic?"

Patty laughed. "Remember where we live, Rick. It takes a day just to get to the Portland airport."

"Yea, but why not Medford? It's half as far."

"Agreed," Patty said, "but you're apt to have more stops, resulting in the same amount of time spent in airports and in the air as you'd spend driving to Portland."

"I guess driving to Portland's not so bad," Rick said. "I'd rather do that than deal with their traffic jams."

Patty smiled. "We choose to live here, in part, because it's somewhat remote and the weather is better than most areas of the country. The only real downside is trying to leave."

Rick agreed. "You're right about that. So if I heard correctly, you'd like Barbara and me to join you all next Sunday?"

"Yep," Patty said. "Can you come?"

"I wouldn't miss hearing about a cruise that takes three days just to get to the port of departure. I'll ask Barbara when I see her this evening."

Rick and Patty climbed into the unmarked car, with Rick at the wheel. "Want to stop for lunch before heading back to the office?" he asked.

"Sure. Do you have a place in mind?"

The car rocked and rolled a bit as Rick drove back toward the Chetco River North Bank Road. "I'm surprised our deceased lived out here, considering the condition of this road. These potholes must make it near impossible to drive after a good rain."

Patty agreed. "It would be pretty dangerous and would deter most people. Makes me wonder why someone drove all the way to the house, killing the victim before leaving."

"Yeah. Maybe we'll find the answer," Rick said before changing the subject back to lunch. "How about the Hungry Clam? The service is fast, and I'm in the mood for calamari."

Patty smiled at how quickly Rick's mind could switch back to food. "Works for me."

# Chapter 2

Turning back onto Highway 101, they crossed the Chetco River Bridge and were about to turn off toward the harbor when the radio crackled. A burglary-in-progress had just been reported not far from the harbor. The sheriff's deputies were tied up with a crash at the north end of the county and asked if Brookings PD could take the call. Patty responded to let dispatch know that she and Rick were on their way.

A young man opened the front door as the detectives pulled up to the run-down house. There were three cinderblock steps leading up to the door, and the windows were covered on the inside with some kind of black material.

"How ya do'n?" he asked as the detectives stepped out of their car.

"Did you report a burglary?" Patty asked.

"I sure did," he said, moving from one foot to the other.

"You called 911 and said that the burglary was happening now," Patty said.

The man at the door looked down at his feet as he rocked back and forth. "Yeah, I might a said that. But there's no one here but me."

Patty used her radio to let dispatch know that the burglary was cold and not in progress as reported. She then continued her questions as Rick took notes.

"What's your name?"

"Lane Granger," he said.

"Anything taken?" Patty asked.

The young man looked a bit disheveled, with his shirt buttoned up wrong and dirty tennis shoes untied. He spoke nervously. "Yeah. In one of the bedrooms I had eight pot plants that are gone."

Patty and Rick locked eyes for a couple of seconds, and then Patty continued her conversation with the man. "Okay. Can you describe the plants or the containers they were in?"

The young man stood with his mouth open. "Describe the plants?" he said with sarcasm. "They were green with pointed leaves and were planted in red or brown plastic containers. I don't remember exactly."

"Okay sir. May I have a phone number in the event we need to contact you?"

The man's facial expression changed quickly as he stared at Patty a few moments, seemingly attempting to think of a response. "I don't have a phone," he said.

Looking directly into the man's eyes, Patty asked. "Then how were you able to call dispatch about the theft?"

The man looked left, right, then left and right again. "I used my roommate's cell phone."

Patty looked at Rick and then back at the young man. "Is your roommate at home now?"

"No," the man said. "I came home last night, and when I checked this morning, he was gone."

"Okay sir," Patty said again. "How would you like to be contacted if your stolen items are recovered?"

The young man thought about the question and then answered. "Could you just bring them by the house here?"

Rick placed one of his feet onto the first of the three cinder blocks. "No, we can't do that, but you can walk down to the harbor sheriff's station now and then and check in with them."

The young man looked at both detectives. "Okay, I guess I can do that."

Patty and Rick exchanged glances and walked back to their car.

"I want to stop by the substation and, if there's a PO in, ask about this guy. He's probably in the system."

Rick opened the driver's door, looked at Patty, and said, "Okay. And then let's get lunch."

The detectives walked into the substation and showed their badges to the middle-age woman who greeted them with a smile. "May I help you?"

"Thanks," Patty said as they walked through the swinging door toward the back offices. "Are PO Heart or Larsen here?"

The friendly volunteer responded, "PO Heart is, but she has someone with her right now." Before the volunteer had finished her sentence, a man walked out of the PO's office and back into the reception area. The volunteer smiled. "Well, not anymore. So you can go back." She then turned her attention to the young man who was leaving. "I hope you have a good day."

"Yeah, you too," he replied.

Patty and Rick spoke with Deputy Heart about the call they'd just been on, and, as they expected, the guy was in the system and currently a client on probation.

Deputy Heart slowly shook her head back and forth. "I doubt he'll be dropping in to ask about his stolen plants, but I'll get him in here for a drug test and talk with him about the 911 call. Thanks."

"No problem," Patty said as she and Rick walked out of the office and down the hall to the reception area. The volunteer was now rolling fingerprints for another customer who had just been offered a job with the post office. She stopped long enough to look up at the two detectives. "Have a nice day," she said.

Patty looked back at the volunteer. "Thanks, you have one too."

As they walked away, Patty commented, "Isn't it great that we have citizens who will spend time volunteering for the sheriff's office?"

"Yeah, it is." Rick said. "Now let's get lunch."

Less than five minutes later, they were ordering calamari and tots.

"So," Patty said. "Do you think that guy's roommate had anything to do with the missing pot plants?"

Rick laughed. "Ya think? I hope that whoever it was took them someplace outside of our county. Did you see the new sign on Chetco?"

Shaking her head, Patty said, "Can't miss it. There are people in this town who complain about nothing being done to increase tourism. Why do they think a tourist driving through would want to stop when they see, within a few blocks, several signs advertising pot, including the four-by-four downtown?"

"I actually think they have increased tourism a bit," Rick said.

"You do?" Patty asked, the tone of her voice expressing surprise.

Rick explained. "There seems to be more panhandlers on the street corners than ever before. Brad tells me that he and Chekowsky are stopping two or three times a day to move vagrants out of town. Said he tells these people about the free lunches provided by several churches. Some take advantage of the offer, but many will eat the free lunch and then go find another corner on which to beg. They've got other things to buy with the money they get, and I suspect many know the location of every pot store around town."

Patty stood up. "It's a huge problem across the country, and the differing state and federal laws sure make our job more difficult." Then changing the subject, she said, "I'm going to buy a soda to go with lunch. Do you want one?"

"No thanks."

Patty returned with her soda, sat down, and looked at Rick. "How'd you do that?"

"How'd I do what?" he asked.

"Eat all of your calamari already."

Rick stuck his fork into a couple of tater tots. "Well, I guess I stuck my fork into each piece like this, dipped them into the sauces, and placed them into my mouth, like this," he said before eating the tots.

Patty shook her head. "I've heard that if you eat slowly your stomach has time to communicate with your mind when it's satisfied, and then you'll eat less."

"Why would I want to do that?" Rick asked as he finished his tater tots. "While you eat the rest of your lunch, I'm going next door to get an ice cream. I'll bring it back here. Want one?"

Patty just smiled and shook her head as she popped the top on her diet soda.

After lunch Rick drove them back to the office. "Oh, about getting together Sunday. I asked Barbara and she said she'd love to join us. She asked me to ask you what we can bring."

"Tell her thanks, but Becky and I have it covered. Cooking together is something we've found we both enjoy, so it's our treat. Plan on coming over about four-thirty."

"I'll let Barb know," Rick said. "She's become so busy lately that it will be nice for the two of us to do something together."

"Is the market that good right now?" Patty asked.

"It seems to be," Rick said. "She spends a lot of time at the office and showing property. Though she tries to keep set hours, it seems she's working into the evening a lot lately."

"Hmmm," Patty said. "From what I've learned over the past ten years since buying my house, there seem to be two kinds of real estate salespeople. There are those who are old enough to be retired, and sell real estate for something to do while bringing in a little discretionary income. Then there are those for whom it's a full-time job. The full-timers work long hours, at least for the first several years while they're building their business. Does Barbara want to make selling real estate a career?"

The detectives got out of the car and began walking to their office as Rick answered Patty's question. "Yeah, at least that's what she says now. I've got some vacation time coming up, and I'm hoping she'll join me for a trip up to Hood River. I'd like to do some boardsailing up there on the Columbia."

As they entered the front door of the building, Patty looked back at Rick. "You should probably let her know that now, so that she can plan to have another agent help her out with any sales she'll have in escrow."

"Oh yeah, I guess I should," Rick said as they walked down the hall to their desks.

Patty's phone was ringing when she sat down, and she could see that the call was from the front desk. "O'Toole."

"Detective, I have a Lillian Haven on the phone for you. Says she knows you and wants to report a burglary."

"Okay, put her through."

Hearing the call go through, Patty identified herself. "This is Detective O'Toole. How may I help you?"

"Hello Detective. This is Lillian Haven. I don't know if you remember me, but my son David went to school with Becky."

"Of course, Ms. Haven. How's David doing?"

"He's in his second year at the local junior college and is doing well. After getting his general requirements out of the way, he wants to study law. How's Becky?"

"Becky's doing great, too. She's at OSU and will go to veterinary school after earning her degree. Now, what can I help you with?"

"I'm calling to report a burglary. My husband, Tom, and I had been away for three days and returned home yesterday evening. We didn't notice anything amiss right away but have now discovered that the lock on our slider is broken and that several things are missing, including Tom's gun."

"Okay, Ms. Haven," Patty said before being interrupted by the caller.

"Please call me Lillian, Detective."

"Lillian," Patty continued. "My partner and I can probably stop by in about an hour to take your report. If we can't make it, one of our officers will. Will you be home?"

"Yes. My husband and I will both be here. Thank you."

Patty ended the call and then filled Rick in on it. "We should probably take this since it involves theft of a firearm. You available?"

"Yep," Rick replied. "That gives me a little time to finish my filing."

\*    \*    \*

At their appointment the detectives walked up to the front door of the small yellow house where they were greeted by Dick and Lillian Haven. Mr. Haven opened the door. "Hello Detectives. Thank you for coming. Please come in."

As Patty and Rick entered the modestly decorated home, Patty noticed that there was no alarm keypad on the wall. Ms. Haven was in the living room, where she asked the detectives to please sit down. "This is all very unnerving," she said. "I hope you find the people who did this."

"We hope so too," Patty said. "Do you have a table we can sit around? It will be easier for us to write."

"Of course," Ms. Haven replied as she led the way into their dining room.

Patty noticed the tired look on Mr. Haven's face. "I'm sure this experience has been difficult, but hopefully we'll find your missing items. Please let us know what was taken."

Mr. Haven spoke first. "I had a Glock 19 on my bedside table. It's gone."

Mrs. Haven reached over and took hold of her husband's hand. "I have both a necklace and ring missing. The necklace was silver with a ruby stone that Tom gave me for our twenty-fifth anniversary. The ring had a fire opal in it."

Rick directed his question to Mr. Haven. "Do you have photographs of these items?"

"We may find photographs of me shooting the Glock or of Lillian wearing the jewelry, but we don't have photographs specifically of each item."

"Okay," Patty said. "How did you realize that the slider door lock had been broken?"

Mrs. Haven sat forward in her seat. "I knew the hummingbird feeders would need to be filled, so I went to unlock the door and noticed it was already unlocked."

"So you've touched the lock?" Patty asked.

"Yes. I'm sorry. I was kind of thinking that maybe we'd forgotten to lock it when we left. When I mentioned it to Tom he checked the lock and saw that it was broken."

"That's when I suspected we'd been burglarized," Tom said, "and I told Lil that we needed to take a close look at our belongings to determine whether anything was taken."

Patty put her notepad down on the table. "Are the gun and jewelry all that's missing?"

Mr. Haven looked over at his wife. "We think so."

Patty nodded to give reassurance to the Havens that she understood. "We're going to ask one of the police officers to come by and dust for fingerprints. Please don't touch the lock, jewelry box, or side table until he's done."

Tears formed in Mrs. Haven's eyes, and she put the tissue she'd been holding to her nose. "Do you think we have a chance of getting our things back?"

The detectives looked at each other.

"There's a chance," Patty said, "but it might take a few months. Usually burglars will stay in one area until they figure they've broken in to as many homes as they can without being caught. There have been a few other burglaries within the past couple of weeks. It could be the same person or group of people responsible. Hopefully we'll find a fingerprint of someone who's in the system."

Patty and Rick got up to go when Mr. Haven spoke up again. "How will we know if you catch the thief? Will you call us, or should we call you periodically?"

Rick pulled out his business card and handed it to Mr. Haven. "We'll give you a call if we find your property. You're welcome to give me a call anytime; however, there's little we can do without a fingerprint or identification except to hope that we catch the person or persons responsible, in the act of committing another crime."

"Okay. Thanks detectives."

Mrs. Haven stepped around in front of them and opened the door. "Thank you for coming."

Patty gave her a nod. "We hope to get your property back. Let us know if you think of anything else that may be helpful."

Rick opened the driver's side door while Patty was getting in on the passenger side. Once they were both in the car Rick said, "I guess we have to give them some hope that their items will be found, but the stuff has probably already been taken to Smith River and fenced."

Patty nodded. "You're right, but I guess there's always a chance some pawnshop owner will call it in."

"You know," Rick said, "I'm thinking about the sheriff's comment regarding the recent rash of burglaries. Brad and Chekowsky were on a burglary call when they were asked to help us out with our murder victim. I wonder what was stolen in that case?"

"Why don't you talk with Brad?" Patty said. "I'm ready to call this a day."

The detectives drove the three blocks back to their offices and ran into Brad and Chekowsky as they all arrived at the small city building at the same time.

"Did OSP show up?" Patty asked.

"Yeah," said Brad. "They snapped a bunch of photos, dusted for prints, vacuumed for fibers, boxed the ashtray, and took it with them. They also arranged to have the body transported to Medford for Doc Miller. We've got it all taped and will do a periodic check."

"Thanks Brad," Patty said before entering the building.

Rick stopped to talk with Brad. "You and Chekowsky were on a burglary call when we asked for your help at the murder scene. Were you there long enough to find out what was taken?"

"Yeah. Prescription drugs. The owner figured it was their daughter who lived with them up until recently. She's had drug problems in the past."

"Thanks," Rick said. "It doesn't seem to be linked to the other recent burglaries."

Rick headed for the break room while Patty wrote down her phone messages. When finished, she put on her jacket then looked up to see Rick walking to his desk with a cup of coffee and handful of cookies. He looked over to see Patty staring at his cookies. Rick glanced at what he held. "I can't think on an empty stomach."

"I didn't say anything," Patty replied with a smile.

"No, but I knew what you were thinking. See you tomorrow."

# Chapter 3

The next day, the detectives met with supervisor Karen Gains at her Fred Meyer office. Patty looked up at Ms. Gains and saw a tired looking forty-year-old woman. Her long, straight hair looked like it hadn't been combed and showed a sprinkling of gray. She greeted both detectives with a smile and polite welcome. Patty returned the greeting. "Thank you for making the time to see us."

Karen Gains nodded. "No problem. I want to help if I can."

"That's good," Patty said. "How long did Lola Martin work here?"

"It will be four years in November."

Rick took notes on a small pocket notepad while Patty asked the questions, as agreed before the interview.

"What kind of an employee was she?" Patty asked.

Ms. Gain's facial expression reflected sadness, as though she were thinking of the deceased. "She was a good employee. Always on time and never any problem. It's hard for me to believe she's gone."

"Did she ever say anything to you suggesting she was in trouble? Delinquent loans? Problem relatives? Anyone she was afraid of?"

Karen Gains closed her eyes as though she were concentrating. "She never mentioned anything to me, Detective, but I'm not close to any of the employees I supervise. Our communication has always been about work. I looked at her employment application before you arrived and she listed a brother as her emergency contact. He lives in Reedsport, and I've written down his name and phone number for you."

"Thank you," Patty said as Rick extended his hand to accept the written information from the supervisor. "Have you ever been to Lola Martin's home?"

Without hesitation Karen Gains responded, "No."

"Okay," Patty said. "One last question. The last time we spoke you said that Ben Brown was close to Lola Martin. Is there anyone else you can think of who may have known Ms. Martin other than during work hours, and other than her brother?"

Pushing her hair back out of her eyes, Karen Gains replied that she did not.

Patty stood up, and Rick followed. "Thank you for your time, Ms. Gains. Would you please contact Ben Brown and ask if he can meet with us now? I know it's earlier than our scheduled appointment, but we'd very much appreciate his being available."

"Certainly," she replied to Patty before picking up the phone. A few minutes later, Patty and Rick were shown into another office, where they waited for Mr. Brown.

The detectives sat with their backs against the wall opposite the door and were looking over their notes when employee Brown walked into the room. Ben was a nice-looking guy of average height and weight. He had a round, gold earring in his left ear and, though his hair was cut short and primarily brown, it was obviously dyed blond on the top of his head. He appeared to be a good ten years younger than the deceased.

"Please sit down," Patty said as the young man walked into the office.

"Sure," he said pulling the only remaining chair out from the desk.

"Has Ms. Gains told you why we're here?" Patty asked.

"Yeah," he said looking down at the floor.

"And what have you been told?" Patty asked.

"She said that Lola was dead."

Patty leaned back in her chair to imitate the manner in which the young man was sitting. "How does it make you feel to learn that Lola died?"

"Pretty bad," he said.

Patty realized that they weren't going to get much from Ben Brown without asking him to elaborate on his responses. "Why does it make you feel bad, Ben? What was Lola Martin to you?"

Ben Brown looked up with tears forming in both eyes. "Lola was my friend. She was the only one here that I could talk with. She didn't deserve to die."

"I'm sorry for the loss of your good friend," Patty said. "Had you ever been to Lola's house?"

Ben, now looking at the floor again, moved his head left and right. "Uh, no," he said. "We used to eat lunch together a lot when we worked the same shifts."

Patty looked at Rick and then back to Ben. "Did Lola ever talk to you about other people she knew? Friends or family members who knew her well enough to have visited her at home?"

Ben looked up at the detectives. "Why are you asking me these questions? How did Lola die?"

"We're not yet sure, Ben, and won't be sure until we hear from the medical examiner. We're looking into the possibility that her house may have been burglarized before or after her death."

Ben sat quietly for a few minutes. "She mentioned her brother a couple of times but said that they were pretty much estranged. He was a pot user, and Lola wanted nothing to do with drugs. I think she had someone do work around her house now and then, like a handyman, but I don't know any more than that."

"Did she ever mention the handyman becoming irritated with her?"

The young man closed his eyes and cocked his head to the side. "Well, she did mention having a guy clean her gutters a few months ago, but I don't remember his name. She told me he was kind of creepy."

"Kind of creepy?" Patty asked. "Did she say why she thought he was creepy?"

Ben's voice level increased as though he were irritated. "Well, he kept telling her that if he had a girlfriend like her he'd take good care of her."

"That would make me mad," Rick said. "if some guy was bothering a girl I liked. Did that make you mad?"

Ben thought about the question. "Yeah, it did. But I didn't do anything about it. I knew I'd never be Lola's boyfriend."

"Were you aware of anything valuable Lola Martin had?"

"Valuable?" he asked.

"Yes," Patty said. "Like a gun or jewelry? Maybe money?"

Ben Brown hesitated. "She once told me she had a gun because she was afraid of living alone. I never noticed her wearing much jewelry, so I don't know about that."

"And what about her money, Ben? Did she tell you whether she had savings?"

"No," he said. "She didn't."

"Okay," Patty said. "Just one more question. Where were you July ninth, the day Lola died?"

"Where was I?" Ben asked. "Why are you asking me where I was?"

"Because we need to know," Rick said. "Where were you?"

"I was at home alone. It was my day off."

Rick leaned forward toward Ben. "Did you see anyone? Order a pizza to be delivered? Talk on the phone with anyone?"

"No," he said. "I pretty much stay to myself."

Patty closed the file in front of her. "We appreciate your time here today, Ben. We may have to talk with you again. Is work the best place for us to reach you?"

"Yeah," he said.

Patty and Rick stood up. "Okay, Ben. Thank you for talking with us." Then handing the young man her business card, Patty continued. "Don't hesitate to give us a call if you think of anything else, even if it's something you don't think is important."

Ben Brown got up, turned and walked out of the room. "Okay," he said as he left.

Rick and Patty walked out to the parking lot and toward their unmarked car. "When we get back I'll type up a report on these interviews, if you want to update the LT?"

"I'll do that," she said. "On another note, I received an email this morning from the sheriff. He mentioned again the greater-than-usual number of burglaries, and he's wondering if we've experienced the same in Brookings. I'll let him know about the Havens' house, and about Lola Martin, though we don't know for certain, yet, that anything was taken. I also need to let OSP know that a gun may have been stolen from her house."

"A stolen gun could explain why she was murdered," Rick said.

\* \* \*

At her desk Patty called the sheriff, who picked up on the third ring. "Hey Sheriff. It's Detective O'Toole. So you've had a lot of burglaries?"

"Mostly guns and jewelry," he said. "Seems our guy is pretty careful, so it's been difficult finding prints, and we've not yet identified any specific pattern. Are you aware of an uptick of burglaries within the past three weeks?"

Patty responded. "Rick and I were called out this morning on a personal welfare check and found the woman dead in her home. It's looking like a homicide. She worked at Fred Meyer, and this afternoon we learned from a co-worker that the woman claimed to have owned a gun. We didn't find a gun or anything else of value when we searched the place this morning. She has a brother who we plan to interview, and he may be able to tell us if she had anything of value in her house. I did get a call today about a burglary. The objects taken included a Glock 19 and some of the woman's jewelry. Brad dusted for prints. I'll let you know if we come up with anything."

"Thanks," the sheriff said. "We'll do the same."

Patty ended her call and then heard the familiar chime of her cell phone. "O'Toole," she answered.

"Is this Patty O'Toole?" the male voice asked.

Patty didn't recognize the voice.

"Who's asking?" she replied.

"Patty, this is Luke Mason. I don't know if you remember me, but I'm the brother of your high school friend Kay Mason, and I took you to your junior prom."

The line was quiet as Patty remembered her junior year in high school. She had friends who were both male and female but no boyfriend so-to-speak. Kay was attending the prom with her boyfriend and wanted Patty to go too. So Kay set things up with her brother, who kindly escorted Patty to and from the prom.

After a period of silence she heard Luke speak up again. "Hello? Anyone there?"

"Yeah, hi Luke," she said. "Of course I remember you and your kindness in taking me to the prom. That was over twenty years ago. Has something happened to Kay?"

"No," he said. "Nothing's wrong. It's just that I recently moved to Brookings and thought I'd look you up. So I Googled your name and found that you're a police officer."

Patty interrupted. "Detective," she said.

"Detective," Luke repeated. "I thought maybe we could get together for a drink some evening and catch up."

"Well, Luke, I'm not sure we need to catch each other up on anything since we only knew one another for a few hours at the prom, but I would like to know how Kay is doing. When were you wanting to meet?"

"I get off work at five," he offered. "How about we meet tomorrow at five-thirty or six at the Black Trumpet?"

"I can't make it tomorrow, but I can meet you there Thursday at six."

"Great," he said. "It'll be good seeing you again."

Patty hung up the phone and looked over at Rick, who was watching her. "You have a question?" she asked.

Rick slowly looked back down to the report he was writing. "Not about that phone call. But I do have a question," he said, looking up at her. "When do you plan to go to Reedsport to interview the brother of the deceased?"

"I've set up an appointment for tomorrow at eleven. I'd like you to come with me, if that works for you."

Rick looked down at his calendar. "I have the time." Then looking up at Patty, he said, "We'll be there for lunch. Know of any good restaurants?"

"Well," Patty smiled. "I don't have a specific restaurant in mind; however, there is a stop I want to make while up that way. Do you like tuna?"

"That depends," Rick said. "Are we talking about Charlie or wild Pacific albacore?"

"Definitely not Charlie," Patty explained. "A few miles west of Reedsport is Winchester Bay, where some of the best albacore tuna I've tasted can be purchased at Sportsmen's Cannery on the wharf. Their slogan is 'Catch what you can and we'll can what you catch.'"

"Sounds great," Rick said. "I hope they sell it by the case. What time do you want to leave?"

"We need about three hours. So let's leave here at eight. We should be able to interview the brother, stop by Sportsmen's Cannery, and make it back here by five."

Rick's phone rang. "Works for me," he said before picking up the receiver.

Patty watched as he jotted down a few notes, thanked the person on the other end of the call, and then looked up at her. "That was the OSP crime lab," Rick said. "I left a message this morning asking for an update on fingerprints found at Lola Martin's house."

Patty picked up her coffee cup. "They find anything?"

Rick shook his head. "We may not know for several months."

Patty gasped. "Months?"

Rick nodded. "I'm told it's due to Oregon's backlog of requests to analyze evidence from a number of sources including firearms, fingerprints, and DNA."

"That's hard to believe," Patty said, "considering the money they've received from the state over the past couple of years. I read that Oregon spent more than a million on hiring, bringing the total number of staff, including a number of DNA and biology evidence technicians, to almost fifty. What are they doing all day?"

Rick closed the file. "Well, from what I've been told, the investment into additional technicians is making a difference; however, they are still taking more time than we have. We're going to have to solve this case with something other than prints, and that doesn't leave us much."

# CHAPTER 4

The next day Rick arrived at the office as Patty was finishing a conversation on the phone. When the call was over, she opened the file in front of her. "We'll be meeting with," Patty paused as she read the name in her file, "Spencer Martin, Lola Martin's brother."

"Let's hope he can tell us something useful," Rick said.

"It's good to hope," Patty said. "Let's go."

Rick stood up touched his gun, an automatic gesture before leaving the office, picked up his car keys, and started out the door with Patty.

They started their drive up the coast when Patty's cell phone rang. She answered "Detective O'Toole."

"Hi Mom," Becky greeted. "Got time to talk?"

"Hi Bec. I've got time, but I can't promise the phone connection won't cut out. Rick and I are on our way to Reedsport. If I lose you, what's a good time this afternoon for me to call back?"

"I've got class all afternoon. If the call drops we can talk tonight. I just wanted to let you know that Dean Burnson announced today that on Friday the school is participating in an active shooter exercise. We saw a film on it today."

"That's great," Patty said. "I'm pleased to know that the school is taking precautions, given the tragedies we've seen on the news. I hope they cover the possibilities of violence using weapons other than just firearms."

"They do, Mom," Becky said. "In the film, weapons used included knives and a vehicle. It makes the possibility of an attack seem very real."

"It is real, Bec, and the best way to survive is to practice how to react. Do you know any of the students taking part?"

"Yea, one of them is in my physiology class. I don't know how he found the time. Between class and homework, I'm swamped."

"I know school is keeping you busy now, Bec, but it will be worth it when you graduate and can work every day at something you enjoy."

"I know, Mom. You've told me that a hundred times."

Patty laughed. "Not a hundred," she said. "Well, maybe ninety-five."

"Okay, Mom, gotta go. See you tonight."

"So, what's up with Becky?" Rick asked.

"There's going to be an active shooter exercise at the college on Friday. I think it's great that time's being made for it."

"That's a good thing," Rick said. "So how do you want to play this with Lola's brother?"

"How about I ask the questions and you take a look around," Patty said. "You may find evidence, if the brother's involved."

*  *  *

The detectives walked to the front door of Spencer Martin's house and knocked. The door was opened by a man who looked to be in his forties. "Hello detectives. I'm Lola's brother, Spencer."

Patty answered, "Hello Spencer. I'm Detective O'Toole, and this is Detective Starker. We appreciate your making time for us."

Spencer opened the door a little wider and stepped back. "Sure, no problem. Come in."

Patty and Rick followed Spencer into the living room where Patty sat down on a small couch and Rick took a seat in the chair closest to the hallway. Patty started the conversation. "We're sorry for your loss, Mr. Martin."

Spencer nodded his head and placed his hands palms down on his thighs. "Thanks. Do you have any idea who killed her?"

"No," Patty said, "not yet. We're hoping to learn something from fingerprints that were found."

"You found fingerprints?" Spencer asked. "Well, that's good," he said after a brief pause.

Patty looked down at the notes on her yellow pad. "Tell me, Mr. Martin, do you know anyone who may have had a reason to harm your sister? Someone who expressed to you that they didn't like her, or someone she may have mentioned to you?"

Before Spencer could answer, Rick stood up.

"Do you mind if I use your bathroom?"

"Ah-h-h, I guess not. It's down the hall."

Patty continued the questioning. "You were going to tell me of anyone who might have wanted to harm Lola."

"No one ever told me they didn't like her. She did mention once that some guy she'd hired to help with the yard scared her. That's when she bought her gun. But she didn't say anything more about it."

"You know she had a gun. Do you know where she kept it?"

Acting nervously, the man paused, looking down the hall toward his bathroom. "Well, she once said it was in a box on her closet shelf. I remember because I told her that the gun wasn't going to keep her very safe if she'd have to go to her closet and take it out of a box in order to protect herself."

When he didn't continue and looked again down the hall, Patty asked, "How did she respond to that?"

"Well, she told me I had a point and she'd think about it. I don't know whether she moved it."

Patty asked, "How long ago was this that you and Lola had the conversation about the gun?"

"Well, I guess it was about six months ago, like maybe around Christmas. We only talked once or twice a year, and it was usually around Christmas."

Rick walked back into the room and looked over at Patty, who looked up to catch his glance and a nod. Spencer squirmed a bit in his chair and spoke to Rick. "I'm sure you saw my pot, and you know that it's legal now, right? I'm within my rights."

Patty responded. "We're here to ask questions about Lola's death, Mr. Martin. Do you know if Lola had a bank account or investments?"

"Investments? I don't think Lola even had a savings account. She didn't trust banks anymore than she trusted the government."

Patty asked, "So, as far as you know, Lola was putting no savings away for her future?"

Spencer laughed. "Oh, she put money away okay. Did just like she'd done when we were kids and put it between her mattress and box spring."

The detectives looked at each other, and Rick made a note on his pocket-sized pad. Patty asked, "Mr. Martin, do you have any idea how much money your sister had hidden under her mattress?"

"No, I don't," he said. "But I'm sure it was her entire savings."

Patty glanced at Rick and then continued the questionning. "This is important, Spencer. Do you recall telling anyone else about your sister's savings?"

Spencer shook his head. "No, I don't talk about my sister to my friends."

"You don't think you told anyone, but is it possible you let it slip out after smoking some of that legal pot?"

Spencer's voice took on a bit of anger. "I wouldn't say anything that would have hurt Lola. She was the only family I had, and I loved her."

Patty nodded. "I understand, but your use of marijuana suggests that you know others who also like to use it. You must know that some people find it addictive, so addictive that they've been known to commit a crime, even kill for the money to supply their habit. So, are you sure that you know of no one who may have had reason to kill your sister?"

Spencer looked a little confused. "I can't think of anyone, but if I do, I'll let you know." He then stood up. "Are there any more questions?"

"Just one," Patty said. "Where were you July ninth, the day Lola Martin was killed?"

"I was here in my home!"

"Is there anyone who can corroborate that, Mr. Martin? Did you have a pizza delivered? Talk with anyone on the phone?" Patty asked.

"No. I don't socialize much. I was here by myself, probably watching T.V."

"Okay," Patty said. "We have to ask you not to leave the state until we tell you otherwise."

"I'm not planning a vacation. Any more questions?"

Patty and Rick stood and began walking to the door. "No," Patty said. "Thank you for your time."

Spencer opened the door for the detectives and stood quietly as they walked to their car.

Rick drove while Patty made a couple of notes. He glanced over at his partner. "Think he knows more than he's telling us?"

Patty paused for a moment. "I think he does, but depending upon the amount of pot he smokes, he may not remember. I'm hoping he'll give it some thought."

"Yeah. We need a break on the case," Rick said. "But for now, let's go buy our tuna and then get some lunch."

Patty smiled, "Works for me."

# Chapter 5

Patty and Rick drove back to the office after making their stops. Walking to their desks, she paused. "I'd better go let the LT know about our interview." Rick nodded and continued on to his desk. Patty spoke again before he sat down. "Hey, Rick, how about confirming with OSP that they checked under the bed mattress."

"I'll give them a call," he said before Patty left the room.

The lieutenant, seeing Patty walk up to his office door, called out, "Come in O'Toole. How'd the interview go?" In fifteen years at the Brookings PD, Patty had never heard him use first names.

The detective pulled out a chair opposite her lieutenant. "Lola's brother confirmed his sister had a gun and came up with additional information that just might explain why someone broke into her house. Seems her way of saving was stashing what may have been a substantial amount of cash under her mattress."

"Did OSP mention anything about having searched the entire bed?" asked the lieutenant.

"They didn't say anything to us. Rick's giving them a call now. The brother didn't think he'd told anyone else about the money, but he's a pot smoker and could have spoken about it while not thinking straight."

"Do you think the brother is good for it?" asked the lieutenant.

Patty shook her head. "It's too early to tell. He seems to genuinely have loved his sister making it difficult to believe that he would have intentionally told anyone about the money, knowing they might harm Lola to get it. We asked him to give us a call if he thinks of anyone to whom he may have mentioned her manner of saving."

Patty thanked the lieutenant for his help and returned to her desk as her cell phone began to ring.

"It's Doc Miller," Patty said to Rick after looking at the caller ID. "Hello Doc," she greeted.

"Hello Detective. I understand you and Rick found the woman OSP dropped off for me."

"That was us, Doc. Is it Lola Martin?"

"Confirmed with her fingerprints," said the doctor. "No need to put a family member or good friend through the difficult identification process."

"Glad to hear that, Doc. Did the blow on her head kill her?"

"It did. I've found no other sign of physical abuse, no sign of struggle, and no evidence of sexual activity prior to or after death. Her clothes aren't torn either. Looking at the photos OSP sent over, it appears that she was bludgeoned elsewhere in the room and then placed on the bed. Does that jibe with what you and Rick found?"

"Yes it does. We're thinking that the killer may have been someone who knew her, or at least cared enough not to leave her on the floor. We've found no apparent reason for the break-in, and everyone who knew the victim is shocked to learn of her brutal death."

"That's why we have detectives, Patty. You and Rick will straighten this out, I'm sure. How's Becky doing? Hard to believe fifteen years have passed since I first met you two. She must be halfway through her degree program."

"Thanks for asking, Doc. Bec has two years left. She still has her sights on becoming a veterinarian and specializing in forensics. We're hoping she'll get a scholarship next year that will cover some of her tuition. Do you know what it costs nowadays to go to grad school?"

Dr. Miller laughed. "Yes, I do, and it's a lot more than what I paid twenty-five years ago. But then young people are earning a lot more today than I did then. Has Becky considered talking to anyone about an internship? If there's no one out there, I have a friend who might be able to intern her for the summers."

"Thanks again," Patty said. "She's received an offer from a vet here in Curry County to intern for both her summers before and after graduation. Becky's pretty excited about it. I'll let her know of your offer though. It's very kind of you."

"Nothing too kind about it. My friend would be forever thankful if I referred a smart, hard-working student like Becky to her. Tell Becky I'm sure proud of her and wish her lots of exciting experiences in her field."

"Thanks again, Doc. I'll tell her. I hope you're making time for R & R during your busy schedule."

"R & R?" Dr. Miller asked. "Every time I think I'll break for vacation, another body is brought in. Klamath County homicides have gone up over the past few years, and the number of fatal automobile accidents since the advent of marijuana sales has also increased. Southern Oregon may have to consider hiring another medical examiner."

Patty sighed. "I'm sorry to hear that. It's frustrating to know that kids are smoking pot as though it has no harmful effects. I read where the human brain continues to form into the mid-twenties. Is that your understanding?"

"It is, Patty. Which means that many young people inhaling pot risk losing some of their mental potential. We're beginning to see the results of marijuana legalization but I don't expect we'll know the long-term effects for another twenty-to-thirty years."

"That's a long wait," Patty said. "Becky and I have had our disagreements, but I feel fortunate to have a daughter with no interest in experimenting with drugs, other than in the lab."

"Your Becky's a smart kid."

"Thanks, Doc. I think so too. Well, it's always good talking with you."

"Sure, Patty. Hope you and Rick soon find whoever took the life of your victim. I'll send you the full autopsy report."

Ending the call, Patty filled Rick in on the details as he stood at the window looking out at the parking lot. He nodded and then looked toward the flag being blown about. "Looks like the wind has picked up in just the past few minutes. One minute the flag's lying still and the next minute it's blowing like crazy."

Patty smiled. "Yeah, that's why we say if you don't like the weather in Brookings, wait a few minutes."

"So, do you think OSP is taking an active role in finding Lola Martin's killer?" Rick asked.

"Probably not," Patty said. "It's too small a case for them to put the manpower into. They agreed we'd work it together, so let's you and me get it solved. We should review what we have thus far."

Sitting back down at his desk, Rick took a yellow-lined tablet out of a drawer, picked up a pencil, and started the list. "We've got a female found alone in the house, dead from a blow on the back of her head."

"And we know by the blood stains," Patty said, "that the woman was probably bludgeoned in the corner of the master bedroom and then either caught by the killer before hitting the floor, or fell to the floor and was then picked up. Either way, he wiped up blood off the floor and laid our victim on the bed."

"And," Rick added. "We know from the ME's report that, other than hitting her on the head, the killer didn't abuse her."

"There's something else we learned from Doc's report," Patty said. "The victim had no signs of having struggled. Her skin had not been scratched, and nothing was found under her fingernails."

Patty put the pencil down. "That would suggest that Lola was not expecting the blow to her head or may not have seen her killer." Patty tapped her pencil against the side of her favorite coffee cup. "What if the killer didn't intend to kill Lola? What if he or she went into the house for some other reason and was surprised to find Lola there?"

Rick nodded. "That might explain why, other than the fatal blow, he didn't harm her. He may have just wanted her money and gun, unless there was something else she had that the killer was after."

Patty stood up. "I'm concerned that if the guy really didn't go in to harm her, we may find that he has no prior record, and therefore running the fingerprints through AFIS won't help. I'll let the LT know about Dr. Miller's call and our interviews." She walked down the hall to the lieutenant's office. The windows on either side of the office door were covered with venetian blinds that were open enough for the lieutenant to see who was at the door.

"Come on in, Detective O'Toole," he called. The lieutenant hand-gestured toward one of the chairs as she walked through the door. "How are you and Rick progressing with the murder investigation?"

"Well, LT," Patty started. "We've got little to go on toward finding our suspect. I spoke earlier today with Doc Miller, and it seems that whoever killed this woman may have done so for reasons other than to make her suffer." Patty filled the lieutenant in on her conversation with the doctor and the facts as she and Rick had noted thus far. "We're thinking that since she was carefully laid upon the bed rather than being left on the floor, whoever killed her may not have intended to do so when he entered the house."

"That could be," said the lieutenant. "You might also consider that whoever killed her did so out of anger and broke in for no other reason than to kill her. Crimes of anger or passion are often committed by a former lover or want-to-be lover. Or a friend or relative who feels betrayed but is then remorseful enough afterward to either clean up the corpse or place the corpse in a position that the killer thinks is making the deceased more comfortable."

Patty listened. "I see what you're saying. We'll run down our list of clues considering all possible motives."

The lieutenant sat back in his chair and folded his arms across his chest. "You hear anything from OSP?"

"Nothing yet, but then that's not really a surprise. We'll continue to work the case at our end."

Patty left the lieutenant and walked down the hall. Entering her office, she saw that Rick was clearing off his desk for the day. He looked up when Patty walked in. "I spoke with the OSP detective on the case, Detective Jackson, and he said they pulled the mattresses off the bed and found nothing. I explained the reason for our asking, and he was glad to know of at least one reason why the woman may have been killed."

"He mention anything about the fingerprints?" Patty asked.

"Negative," Rick said. "They're still waiting."

"Okay," Patty said. "Let's pick this up again tomorrow. Have a nice evening."

"Yea, you too, Patty. See you tomorrow."

# CHAPTER 6

Patty's phone rang and she could see it was her mother. "This is my mom," she said to Rick.

Rick smiled. "Hope all is well with her and Bill."

"Detective O'Toole," Patty said, knowing her mother loved it when she answered that way.

"Hello Detective O'Toole. This is your mother."

"Hi Mom. What's up?"

"Oh, not much. Got any new murders you can tell me about?"

"Nothing I can tell you about, Mom," Patty said with a smile.

"Well," Maggie said, "in that case I'll tell you what's up with Bill and me."

"I'm listening, Mom."

"Well, we're thinking of buying a condo together."

"You're what?" Patty asked. "Mom, you've only known Bill for a couple of years. I think it's great that you enjoy each other's company, but buying a condo together? I think that's rushing things a bit. You don't even live together now."

"Funny you should mention that, Patty, because I was thinking the same thing. I mean, if we really care for each other we ought to be living together. So I'm moving in with Bill next weekend."

There was a long pause during which nothing was said between mother and daughter. Rick stopped writing while hearing Patty's side of the conversation and could tell her blood pressure was rising by the red showing up in her cheeks.

"Okay, Mom. I think we should have a quiet, adult conversation about this, and now is really not the time. Will you be home tonight? I'll be a little late but should be there by seven thirty. I think it would be great if we sat down together after dinner and talked about this."

Rick thought that he could see smoke coming out of Patty's ears.

"Of course, dear. I always enjoy our talks, and tonight after dinner would be wonderful. I'll let Bill know that I'm having dinner with you and Becky."

"Okay, Mom. I'll see you tonight. Until then, please don't discuss this any further with Bill. Please just wait until we can discuss it together this evening. Can you do that, Mom?"

"Oh, Patty, you sound like you did when you were ten years old and I wanted to dress up for Halloween to go trick-or-treating with you. Remember? You were Little Miss Muffet and I was going to be a sheep. You didn't like the idea of me gluing cotton balls all over my leotard and wearing a sign that said Ba-a-a-a. You were so cute when you were mad."

Rick, who wasn't sure if Patty was going to make it through the call, pulled open one of his desk drawers and pulled out a bottle of water that he set in front of his partner.

"Mom, let's talk this evening. I have to go."

"Okay, dear. But before you go I must say that I detect a bit of stress in your voice. It doesn't bother me though, because just the other day I read an article about stress and how good it is for you. The trick is to believe that stress is a normal part of life. Your life has meaning when you're stressed because you're usually stressed out about people and activities in life that you care about. Doesn't that make you feel better, Patty dear?"

"I'll see you at home for dinner tonight, Mom. I've got to go now."

"Okay dear. Love you."

Patty took a swig of water from the bottle Rick had placed on her desk. "Love you, too, Mom."

When Patty hung up the phone receiver Rick suddenly picked up his pencil and looked down at his notes.

"Do you want to comment?" Patty asked.

Rick paused. "Yeah," he said. "Let's take a drive out to the golf course in a while and get some lunch. A nice drive in a peaceful setting might be good today."

# CHAPTER 7

After writing reports most of the day, Patty sat at her desk tapping a pencil, causing Rick to look up. "It's five o'clock and you seem pretty deep in thought. Thinking about the case?"

"No," Patty said. "I'm supposed to meet Luke at six at the Black Trumpet."

Rick put his file down. "Have I heard about this guy?"

"Yeah, he's the brother of my high school girlfriend. He took me to the junior prom and called last week to meet up."

Rick smiled. "You don't seem too interested."

Patty shrugged. "I'm not. I agreed to meet him because he did a kind thing taking me to the prom, but that was almost twenty years ago. I guess I figure I owe him this drink, but there's something about him that makes me a little uneasy."

Rick stood up to put his jacket on. "Maybe you should call it off. I can assure you that no guy is going to think a girl owes him a drink years after he took his sister's classmate to a high school prom."

"Well, maybe I'm just giving it too much thought," Patty said. "He's probably just trying to be friendly. I guess I would like to know how his sister's doing."

Rick pushed his chair back up to the desk. "Well, okay. You can let me know tomorrow if he wants to dance with you again."

Patty smiled. "Not going to happen. Have a good evening."

"You too," Rick smiled. "See you tomorrow."

Patty took out her cell phone and called Becky. "Hi Bec. Just want to remind you that I'll be late getting home this evening."

"Oh yeah," Becky said. "Tonight's your date with that guy who took you to the prom."

"It's not a date, Bec. Just a drink with the brother of an old high school friend. I should be home by seven thirty."

"Okay, Mom. If you say so."

"I say so, Becky O'Toole, and I can hear in your voice that you're trying very hard not to laugh. I'll see you tonight."

At five forty-five, Patty put her files away and took a few minutes to freshen up before driving over to meet with Luke Mason, who was already seated at a corner table in the restaurant when Patty walked in.

"Hi Patty," he said with a grin, walking toward her as she came through the door.

Patty quickly extended her hand. "Hi Luke."

Luke shook Patty's hand. "I was hoping for a hug, but a handshake will do for now."

Patty sat down with her back against the wall, and Luke stepped around to sit next to her as he dragged his glass across the table.

"I'd rather you sat across from me," she said while pushing the glass back to where it was. "It'll be easier to talk."

Luke stepped back and pulled a chair up to the table. "No problem," he said. "Whatever makes you comfortable."

A waitress walked up and Luke asked, "What would you like to drink?"

Patty looked up at the waitress, "I'll have a glass of Cabernet."

"Make that two," Luke said.

After a moment of silence, Patty spoke. "So, Luke, tell me about Kay. How is she doing? Last I knew, she'd moved to California and we've not been in touch since."

"Kay is doing great. She married a Navy guy and they live in Lemoore, California. She has a couple of kids and works part time. Do you have children?"

Patty smiled. "I have a daughter. What about you?"

Rather than answer the question, Luke asked, "Maybe you and your daughter would like to come over to my place for a barbecue. What about this Saturday?"

Before Patty could respond, the waitress arrived with their wine. When she stepped away from the table, Patty answered Luke. "I'm afraid that won't work for me, Luke. My daughter and I both keep pretty busy."

Luke smiled. "Oh, no problem. I understand. Maybe another time?"

"Oh," Patty said. "We'll see. So, tell me about yourself. What kind of work do you do?"

"Well," he said, "I work for AT&T. My territory includes all of Curry County, so I do a lot of travelling."

"That sounds interesting. How long have you worked for them?"

"About ten years," he said. "They transferred me here when the prior rep for this area left the company."

Patty sipped her wine. "Maybe you can answer a question for me."

Luke sat up a little straighter. "Sure. What do you want to know?"

"There are times when my phone rings and the person calling will ask 'Is this Ms. O'Toole?' to which I used to respond, 'Yes'. Then, one of two things would happen. Either the caller would repeat their question or there would be silence. After a couple of these calls it was clear to me that the caller was a telemarketer. What I want to know is how does the caller benefit if I haven't bought anything? Do you know the kind of call I'm talking about?"

Luke nodded and looked eager to respond. "I know exactly what you're talking about. The caller wants you to talk so that they can replicate your voice and use it to make purchases without your knowledge. The key is to talk as little as possible and never to say the word *yes*."

Patty took another sip of wine. "That's information the public should have. I'll certainly be sharing it. Thank you."

"Oh, no need to thank me," he said. "I'm enjoying talking with you." Then seeing their wine glasses empty, Luke looked up for the waitress. "Let's have another glass of wine. There's still a lot I'd like to know about you and your exciting career."

Patty stood up and took her purse off the back of her chair. "No thanks, Luke. I really need to be going home. It was nice of you to buy me the wine, and I hope you'll say hello to Kay for me next time you talk with her."

"I'll walk you out to your car," Luke said as he left money on the table and walked with Patty to the door. Once outside the restaurant he asked, "When can I see you again? I know you're busy, but maybe we could do this again. Like Thursdays could be our wine evenings."

Patty opened her car door and responded before climbing in. "No, Luke, I've enjoyed our talk this evening, but I don't want to go out again. I'm just too busy to date."

"Oh, no problem," he said. "But I'll give you a call sometime just in case you change your mind."

Patty drove off and through her rearview mirror watched Luke walk to his car.

# Chapter 8

It was seven thirty when Patty walked into her house. "Hi Mom!" she heard Becky yell from her bedroom. Patty walked to Becky's bedroom door, finding her seated at her desk and studying. "Hi Bec. What are you studying?"

Becky answered without looking up from her book. "Physiology for a test tomorrow."

"Did you want dinner?" Patty asked.

"No. I've snacked most of the day, so I'm not hungry."

"Okay. I'll go heat something up."

Becky turned around to look at her mom. "How'd it go?"

"A nonevent," Patty said.

"Oh," Becky said, and then added, "Grandma's in the kitchen."

Patty nodded to Becky and then walked into her bedroom, where she took her gun out and laid it carefully on top of her nightstand. She took off her shoes, put on bedroom slippers, and padded back down the hall to the kitchen.

Maggie O'Toole was seated at the table. "I made a meatloaf and prepared a plate for you. It's in the fridge."

Patty walked over to the refrigerator, took out the plate, set it in the microwave, and pushed the buttons for two minutes. She then poured herself a glass of milk and prepared her place setting at the table.

"You wanted to talk?" her mother asked.

The microwave went off and Patty took the plate out, set it on the table, and sat down. "Tell me about Bill, Mom," she said before taking a bite of the dinner.

"Tell you about Bill?" Maggie asked. "You know Bill."

Patty set her fork down. "No, Mom. I really don't know Bill. This is what I do know. I know that he's taken you on a cruise, a trip during which you spent most of your time alone because he wanted to gamble. I know that the two of you have traveled to places you'd not before visited, and had a wonderful time. I know that he's polite and has been very nice when I've been with the two of you."

Maggie folded her hands on the table. "Well, there you are, Patty. What is it you don't like?"

Patty took a couple more bites of dinner, drank half the glass of milk, and put her fork down again. "I also know that the two of you have only known each other for two years and that during that time you've either been gone together on trips or he's been gone to poker tournaments. How do you know what it's like to be at home with Bill for at least a six-month period? I also know that he has a daughter who has not yet made the time to meet you."

Maggie unfolded her hands and set them in her lap. "You're worried about me, Patty, and I love you for it. The thing is, there will never be another man for me like your father, and I believe Bill knows that. I don't need a man around me all the time, Patty. I have my friends and hobbies that I don't want to give up any more than Bill wants to give up his gambling. We've discussed his gambling and it's not a crutch for him. He's a very intelligent man and gambles because he enjoys the challenge, and he wins."

Patty looked her mother in the eyes. "How do you know his winnings during these past couple of years aren't just a lucky streak? How do you know that his luck won't change and he'll lose whatever he has?"

"Well," Maggie said, "I don't know. But it's important that you know that I have my own money, and Bill knows that I won't gamble with it. You should also know that I'll be paying half the rent when we move in together, and that's something he argued with me about and on which I was insistent."

Patty continued to eat her meatloaf while shaking her head. "I don't know, Mom. It just seems too soon."

Maggie sat up straight and looked at her daughter. "Patty, I don't expect you to understand, but when you're my age you will. None of us knows if we have one day or ten years left on this planet. When your father died I figured life was over for me too. Oh, I enjoy my friends and our get-togethers, but nothing was ever exciting. Bill has brought excitement back into my life again. He genuinely enjoys my company, and he doesn't ask for anything I'm not willing to give."

Patty set down her fork and pushed her plate back. "But . . ."

"No Patty," Maggie said. "I know you're worried, but I'm asking you to trust me. You've always told Becky that you'll trust her unless she does something to break that trust. I'm asking you to grant me the same consideration. I'm asking you to let me enjoy this time I have with Bill."

Patty pushed her chair back, walked around the table, and gave her mom a big hug. "Okay, Mom. I love you, and I do trust you to make good decisions. Just know that I'm available if you ever want to talk, and your room is always here if you want to come home."

"I love you, too, dear," Maggie said before standing to leave the room.

Patty looked lovingly at her mother. "You going to bed?"

"No," Maggie said with a broad smile on her face. "I'm going to pack my bag. Bill's picking me up in twenty minutes."

Patty stood motionless as Maggie left the room. Then talking quietly to herself, she said, "Hmmmm. Who led that conversation?"

# CHAPTER 9

Sunday evening Maggie, Bill, Rick, and Barbara congregated in the living room at Patty and Becky's home. Once everyone was situated with a drink, Becky asked her grandmother and Bill to tell everyone about the cruise.

"We'd love to," Maggie said. "The cruise was an enjoyable experience and an education about the government and tax systems of other countries. Do you want to hear about the sights we saw or what we learned about the cost to live?"

Patty smiled. "Let's hear about the living costs first, so that you can end with your descriptions. I'll bet it was beautiful."

Bill nodded in agreement. "We learned a lot that served to remind us of why we choose to live in the U.S., even though it's not perfect. I wish every young person was required to take a high school course that would teach the facts about living in these countries other than solely their recreational vacation highlights."

Barbara chimed into the conversation. "I'm interested in the cost of real estate."

"Well," said Maggie, "the cost depends upon the neighborhood in which you live, as it does here. The problem for young adults everywhere is trying to save up enough money for the down payment. England, Scotland, Ireland, and

Iceland are all countries in which the residents are highly taxed. The income-tax rate in Iceland is 46.30 percent. They also pay a value-added tax, or VAT, of 11 to 24 percent, depending upon the product purchased."

"Wow!" Rick said. "I've heard many times about how great these countries are because of the free education and medical care. We don't hear about the taxation."

"No we don't," Bill agreed. "But it's logical that the money for free services has to come from some source. In one or more of these countries residents may have to pay for some of their medication, and for healthcare other than emergencies, the wait to see a doctor can be much longer than it is here."

"Okay, time to cheer up. Let us tell you about the beauty we saw," Maggie said cheerfully. "Bill has photos he'll pass around as we talk. The countryside was beautiful everywhere we visited, and both Scotland and Iceland have fabulous waterfalls. England has acres and acres of bright green valleys. Scotland also has beautiful rock hill formations that created, for us, some of our favorite countryside views. Iceland is green but it's different. The shade of green is a yellow green and the foliage is moss that grows on the rocky hillsides, much of which is volcanic rock. It's called the island of fire and ice because of its many volcanoes and glaciers.

"Claire and I went on an Alaskan cruise, about . . . fifteen years ago," Rick said. "We saw spectacular glaciers."

Bill nodded with understanding. "These are much different. The Iceland glaciers are not like those in Alaska where the ship pulls into a fjord close to a two-hundred-foot wall of ice that calves as you watch. In Iceland we saw the glaciers from a distance, and they weren't much higher than sea level."

"Did you see any castles?" Barbara asked.

"We did," Maggie said. "The countries of England, Scotland, and Ireland are all a lot older than the US, and much of their architecture dating back many hundreds of years has been preserved. Seeing real castles and walking around churches that are hundreds of years old was an experience in itself. The Canterbury Cathedral was built in about 1050 AD, and was spectacular!

"Did you see many young people?" Becky asked.

"We saw lots of young people," Maggie replied. "Far more than we're used to seeing here in Curry County."

As a matter of fact," Bill added, "in Iceland all we saw were young people, and much of their country's history and most of their landscape is the subject of a saga or tale."

Maggie continued the explanation. "The trolls that Americans have read about in nursery rhymes are real figures, even in today's Icelandic culture. Our tour guide explained that fear is instilled in Icelandic children early in life by using the threat of trolls and past gruesome experiences to keep children aware of their surroundings, which include deep crevices hidden by thin veils of moss. In one downtown area there are statues of two giant trolls that are replicas of the parents of Santa Claus."

Patty interrupted in order to invite everyone to the dinner table and asked Rick if he'd pour the wine.

"We've got coffee too," Patty offered.

"Coffee would be great," said Bill.

"I'd love a cup of coffee, too, dear." Maggie said. "May I help you?"

"I'll help," said Becky, following her mother into the kitchen. "Please hold off on talking more about your trip until Mom and I can hear too."

After Patty and Becky joined everyone again at the dinner table, Bill complimented the chefs. "This looks delicious!"

"And smells heavenly," Maggie added.

"Thanks," Patty and Becky said in unison, then Becky added, "Mom and I worked together on the lasagna and salad, and the garlic bread is from Freddy's."

"Good old Fred Meyer," Rick said. "I learned soon after moving here that if they don't have it at Freddy's, you don't need it."

"I like to think of the store as our very own indoor mall," Maggie said with a smile.

"Maybe I'll use that line with new clients," Barbara said, laughing. "It might take the sting out of telling them about the two-and-a-half hour drive to the nearest Macy's."

After the prayer, Maggie suggested that before she and Bill went on about their trip, Barbara should talk about her work. "Barbara, tell us what's happening in the real estate market these days."

"Well, the market is still quite good except for those homes priced over a million. They don't sell near as frequently as homes in the two- to five-hundred thousand-dollar range. Of course, oceanfront homes still command a premium when they do sell. The rental market remains tight, making it very difficult for newcomers to our area. This has been a real problem for the hospital as they continue their effort to recruit new medical personnel."

Maggie took a sip of her coffee and then put the cup down. "I hadn't realized that we had such a rental shortage."

"You know, Maggie," Bill said, "there's lots more that we could tell about our trip, but we should save some of it for our next gathering."

Maggie nodded. "I agree, but before we stop I'd like to tell everyone about the Icelandic sheep."

"The sheep?" Becky asked.

"Yes, dear. Everywhere we looked along the countryside, we saw sheep gathered in groups of three. It was quite puzzling until we asked the guide and she explained. The rams are owned to mate, not unlike the reason for stud horses. They even have pedigrees like horses and can be very expensive to purchase. So, the ram and ewe mate, and when the ewe gives birth, she's allowed to keep two of her lambs. If she gives birth to three, the third is given to be cared for by a ewe without her own lambs. According to our guide, this is done because the ewe cannot sustain more than two lambs, which is why we always saw the sheep in groups of three."

"But that means the father doesn't get to help with the family and see his children grow up," Becky said somewhat solemnly. "That's pretty sad."

"Well," Bill said. "Farming is a business, and one of the ways a sheep farmer makes his money is with his rams. They are continually sold or rented out for the sole purpose of mating."

"We saw sheep all over the countrysides of England, Scotland, and Iceland," Maggie said. In Iceland their groups of three are seen roaming the hills of yellow-green moss. Now and then we'd see a beautiful patch of bright green grass where several sheep would be grazing. Our guide told us that this patch of fresh grass was the last location the sheep were placed to eat in order to fatten up before being slaughtered."

"Oh my gosh," Barbara said with a tone of surprise in her voice.

"Well," Patty chimed in. "On that happy note, who would like dessert? Becky made a great lemon-meringue pie."

"I can't pass that up," Rick said.

"Nor can I," followed Bill.

Maggie addressed her granddaughter. "I love your pie, Bec, but I'm quite replete at the moment, so I'll have to pass. I would love to take a small piece home with me to enjoy with coffee tomorrow morning."

"You've got it, Grandma. Pie for you Barbara?"

"Oh yes. I'm afraid you've baked my favorite, and no amount of willpower will keep me from enjoying a slice."

"Bec and I will be right back with pie," said Patty as she and Becky walked into the kitchen.

Becky started cutting the pie while her mother took dessert plates out of the cupboard. "I guess the animal world can be as cruel as humans." Becky said. "Separating the ewe and lambs from the ram just doesn't seem right."

Patty set down the plates and took dessert forks out of the drawer. "Well, Becky, there's a lot to raising of animals for profit about which we who are not farmers are unaware or don't understand. The sheep have been farmed that way for hundreds of years and may not know any better."

"I guess," Becky said as she transferred several pie slices to the plates.

Becky and Patty distributed the pie, and as everyone began to enjoy their dessert, Maggie was the only one without food in her mouth. "So, Patty and Rick, what's been going on in Brookings while we were gone? Did you catch any bad guys, and if you did, was it anyone I know?"

Patty looked over at Rick, who quickly placed his last piece of pie in his mouth. "Actually," she said, "we're investigating a death that occurred last week. We're working with both OSP and the sheriff. And, no, I don't think you knew her. She was living up the Chetco north bank."

Maggie, always interested in Patty's and Rick's work, leaned forward in her seat. "How old was she? Was she alone at the time? Do you know how she died?"

"We can't talk about the case now, Mom. We don't yet have a suspect, and we hope to soon learn whether OSP found anything after sending the fingerprints to AFIS."

"What's AFIS?" Barbara asked.

Maggie quickly spoke up with a contented smile on her face. "I can answer that question. AFIS is the acronym for the Automated Fingerprint Identification System. You get to know these things when your daughter's a detective."

Barbara laughed. "I'll bet you do. I've learned more about law enforcement activity during the few months Rick and I've dated than I'd ever learned watching television programs. And, I've learned that most of what I see on the T.V. is not realistic."

"Yeah," Rick said. "No one would watch the shows if they were realistic. Too boring."

Barbara set her pie plate down on the table. "This has been wonderful, Patty and Becky. May I help with the dishes?"

"We appreciate your asking," Becky said, "but Mom and I've got this."

"Well, if you're sure," Barbara said and then turned toward Rick. "I hate for us to eat and run, Rick, but I need to stop in at the office before we go home this evening, and prepare a contract for an early morning appointment."

Rick looked surprised as he responded, maybe a little too quickly. "The office? You didn't mention anything about going to the office after dinner. This is supposed to be our time."

"I know," Barbara said quietly. "I forgot. It won't take long, but let's talk about it in the car."

Rick looked at Patty and shrugged his shoulders. "Well, I guess we'd better get going. Good seeing you, Maggie and Bill, and hearing about your trip."

Not long after Rick and Barbara left, Maggie and Bill called it a night too.

"This was wonderful, dear." Maggie said.

Bill hugged the two cooks. "Thanks for a fabulous meal and wonderful evening."

Patty walked her mom and Bill out to their car. "We hope to get together again soon," Bill said. "Next time at our place. I'll barbeque."

"Sounds great," Patty said, as it briefly crossed her mind that he used the term *our place.*

With the guests gone, Patty and Becky cleared the table and worked together on the dishes. Becky rinsed a plate and handed it to her mom to put into the dishwasher. "Do you think Rick and Barbara are going to stay together, Mom?"

Patty hesitated, as she was wondering the same thing. "Well, I don't know. It's hard for a couple to stay together when they each have a career with no consistent work hours. Claire was a housewife and stay-at-home mom once Skylar was born. This allowed Rick to work long hours and be gone when he needed to attend conferences or work on out-of-town cases. Claire had her own interests and friends, but Rick and Skylar came first. I guess it's something Rick and Barbara will have to work out."

# Chapter 10

Patty was already at her desk working when Rick walked in Monday morning. "Great dinner last night," he said. "You and Becky know how to cook!"

Patty looked up and smiled. "Thanks, Rick," she said. "I've always enjoyed cooking with Becky. Gives me some quality time with my daughter."

Patty watched Rick take off his jacket and sit down. "Everything okay with you and Barbara?"

Rick answered with a bit of reluctance. "I guess so. Lately it seems we don't have a lot of time together. I keep telling myself that I just need to be patient but it seems, more and more, that her business is taking up all of her time. She has no set hours and doesn't seem to care how it's affecting us as long as she's writing up offers."

Patty nodded. "Have you thought about what you need, Rick? It's been four years since losing Claire and Skylar, and Claire molded her life to caring for you and your daughter. She enjoyed being home when you were there, regardless of what hours you worked, and she found ways to maintain friends and fill her time alone when you were on the job. Have you asked Barbara about her need to have a man in her life, and how she feels about making some changes in her schedule in order to accommodate time together with you?"

Rick was looking at Patty as though she were speaking an unknown language. "No and no," he said. "Barbara should tell me if she doesn't want or need me."

Patty smiled. "I'm just suggesting that it might be a good conversation for the two of you to have. Remember, Rick, I've been single for the past ten years, so I know a little about searching for the right mate. I learned from a good psychologist that determining what I need before getting into another relationship would save me a lot of grief later on. It's not easy."

"Okay. Thanks. I'll think about what you've said."

Patty nodded as she picked up her pencil. "Okay, let's go over what we know about our suspects in the Haven burglary. Then we'll have time to work on reports and filing."

"We know the point of entry into the house was through the slider," Rick said. "And that a house in Pistol River was broken into the same way a week earlier."

Patty put down her pencil. "No one was in the Pistol River home when it was burglarized. Thus far we know that it was jewelry and a couple of guns that were stolen. We also know that the burglars turned the house upside down, turning furniture over and knocking breakables off the shelves before leaving."

"There's probably a connection," Rick said, but we'll need some kind of a break in order to solve these. The responsible is probably driving around with the stolen property in the back seat of his car. A routine traffic stop by a perceptive officer would help."

Patty nodded in agreement. "Let's switch over to the Lola Martin case for a minute. When I spoke last week with the LT, he suggested something we hadn't discussed."

"What's that?" Rick asked.

"That her murder could have been a crime of passion by a former lover or want-to-be lover."

"I'd wondered about that myself," Rick said. "I certainly saw a lot of homicides for that reason while working in Boston. But we haven't spoken yet with anyone who might fit that description."

"Unless there was more to her relationship with Ben Brown," said Patty.

"We may have to revisit Mr. Brown," Rick said as he stood up. "But for now, it's still two hours before lunch. I'm going to get another cup of coffee and hopefully a doughnut or two. Want anything?"

"No," Patty said. "I'm good."

Rick returned from the break room with coffee and cookies. "This should tide me over till lunch," he said with a smile. "It'll make my report writing a little easier too."

"I'll write up the interview with Karen Gains if you want to take Ben Brown," Patty offered.

"Works for me. I should be able to get it done this morning if we're not interrupted with a call."

*   *   *

After lunch, Patty and Rick drove back to the office. Patty sat down, saw her phone light blinking, and listened to the message.

"That was Spencer Martin," she said. "Seems he now remembers mentioning to someone that his sister stashed her cash under the mattress. He's going to be in Brookings tomorrow and wants to stop in."

"This could be the break we need," Rick said. "Anytime after one works for me."

Patty made the call. "He'll be here at two. I'll go let the LT know."

"Great," Rick said. "I need to spend the next couple of hours on reports. Want to get it done before I go home."

Patty pushed her chair away from the desk. "Yeah. I've got a few things to write up, too." Before Patty stood up the scanner chirped and the detectives heard dispatch send Officer Bradley on a welfare check of an older couple.

Officer Chekowsky spoke up to cover him. Fifteen minutes later the phone on Patty's desk rang.

"Chekowsky and I are at the home of Mary and Thomas Hanley, " Brad said. "We've found a man and a woman both tied up and shot. You and Rick need to get out here."

Patty stood up while nodding to Rick that they had to leave. "We're on our way. Don't let anyone else in the house and don't touch anything."

The detectives arrived at the house and had to ask the growing number of neighbors congregating along the sidewalk to step aside. Chekowsky had already taped off the yard and entrance to the house. "Brad's inside," he said.

The two detectives put a set of booties on their feet and gloves on their hands before walking through the front door and into the living room. There, tied to two chairs, were an elderly man and woman, each shot twice in the chest. Looking about the room, Patty could see that drapes for two slider doors leading to the backyard had been pulled off their tracks, and a lamp lay broken on the floor. "It appears as though the couple gave a bit of a fight," she said. Then, taking a closer look at the slider, she said, "The lock is broken, suggesting this is the point of entry. Let's take a look around for any obvious signs of theft, and then I'll call the LT."

Searching the house, Rick called out, "In here!" Patty walked into the master bathroom where Rick was taking photos. The medicine cabinet was open and on the floor was an empty container labeled codeine. Rick pointed toward the bedroom. "The jewelry box on the dresser appears to have been cleaned out."

"I'll call the LT," Patty said as she walked back into the living room.

The lieutenant had already heard about the murders when he picked up Patty's call. "What do you think?" he asked.

"Looks like a burglary turned robbery," Patty said as she explained what she and Rick found. "We need the Major Crimes Team on this one."

"I agree," said the lieutenant. "You call the sheriff and I'll get a hold of OSP. Who asked for the welfare check?"

"Dispatch said it was Meals on Wheels. Maybe someone there will know if the couple has local relatives."

"Let me know what you find," said the lieutenant.

"Oh, and one more thing, LT. It appears that entry was through the slider where the lock was broken. Rick and I saw the same damage to a slider last week when we responded to a burglary. The homeowners were gone at the time and discovered upon returning that their gun and jewelry were missing. Could be the same suspects who broke in here."

"Could be, O'Toole. And, if it is, they've become a lot more dangerous. Let's talk again when you and Rick get back. By then I'll have spoken with OSP."

"Thanks, LT." Patty said. She shared her conversation with Rick and then called the sheriff, explaining the situation and the need for his help on a Major Crimes Team.

"On my way," he said. "I'll send Ted Kindle and Detective Jones over too."

"Thanks, Sheriff," Patty said before walking over to Rick, who was squatting down looking at a cartridge case on the floor almost hidden by the edge of the sofa.

"Definitely 9 mm," he said. "And from a striker-fired pistol, maybe a Glock."

"They were each shot twice," Patty said. "The perp was either sloppy about picking up his brass, or he left quickly for some reason."

Rick looked up at Patty and smiled.

"What?" she asked.

"Well," he said. "I can't help but note your use of the East-Coast term for a suspect, a term that had been part of my everyday vocabulary when I served for Boston. Maybe part of me is rubbing off on you."

Patty had to smile, too. "Yeah, maybe so."

# CHAPTER 11

The next morning Rick walked in with a bakery bag and walked over to Patty's desk.

"The chocolate old-fashioned is on the top. So, what are your thoughts on the double homicide? Think it's related to the Lola Martin murder?"

Patty paused a moment before taking a doughnut out of the bag. "My gut tells me no. There's no evidence that the person who murdered Lola tortured her in any manner. Clearly in the deaths of the elderly couple, the person or persons involved tied them up, causing a lot of suffering before killing them. Do you think the cases are related?"

"Well," Rick said, "I pretty much agree with you."

Before Patty could take a bite of the pastry, her phone rang. "Mr. Martin," Rick heard her say. Two minutes later Patty hung up. "Spencer Martin's plans have changed. He drove down here yesterday and needs to get back to Reedsport for a doctor's appointment late this afternoon. Okay with you if I tell him to come on in now."

Rick took a sip of coffee out of the Styrofoam cup. "Sure. Let's hope he's got a good lead. It would be nice to get a break on this case."

Patty nodded. "Yeah, considering we're not going to get results on the fingerprints anytime soon."

Officer Bradley walked in to the office and up to Rick's desk.

"What's up, Brad?" Rick asked.

The officer handed Rick a report. "You asked me to check on whether there were footprints found at the Havens' house that matched those at the home of the murdered elderly couple."

"They a match?" Rick asked.

"Well, the Havens have a concrete patio leading up to their back slider, the point of entry."

Rick tapped his pencil. "So you didn't find anything?"

"Let me finish," Brad said. "The sprinklers must have been on not long before the burglary took place, creating a muddy area where the grass is thin. Looks like someone was trying not to get his shoes too muddy and stepped on the ball of his foot in the mud before stepping onto the concrete patio. It's only the ball of the right foot, but it's consistent with the others and looks like a match. An OSP criminalist will have to officially confirm it."

Rick glanced at Patty before thanking Brad. "Good work," he said.

Patty nodded to Brad, who then left the office.

Rick looked puzzled. "How'd they get the state to work so fast on the footprints when we're still waiting on results of the fingerprints we sent them?"

"The results didn't come from the state," Patty said. "A couple of the sheriff's deputies who took photos of the prints at our homicide scene also made casts and compared the casts to those made by Ted up on Pistol River. They must have made a cast of the print found at the Havens' too."

"Wow!" said Rick. "That's good work!"

"It is," Patty agreed. "We've now got three homes that were probably burglarized by the same one or more suspects," she said. "Could be the only reason there hasn't been another murder is because the residents weren't home." Patty picked up her pencil and pulled her tablet across the desk. "Give me the dates of those three break-ins."

Rick opened the files on his desk. "The Pistol River burglary was July tenth. Sometime between July eighth and eleventh the Havens were burglarized. The ME figures the double homicide occurred July seventeenth."

Patty looked at her calendar. "July tenth and seventeenth were Sundays. The break-in at the Havens' could have been on Friday, Saturday, or Sunday. Let's assume for now that it was Sunday."

Rick looked up at Patty. "You thinking the suspects knew the victims weren't home?"

"I am, Rick. Spencer Martin should be coming in any minute now. When we're done with him, find out if any of our victims attend church, and if they do, what church and what day and time. Meals on Wheels might know the church habits of our deceased couple."

"You may be onto something there, Patty. I'll also find out if there was a reason why our murdered couple was home if their regular habit was to attend a church service Sunday morning."

Patty's phone rang and the front desk let her know that Spencer Martin had arrived. "Thanks. I'll come get him," she said. "He's here," she said to Rick. "I'll bring him back to the interview room."

Rick left his desk and walked down the hall while Patty greeted Lola's brother, who was seated in one of three chairs in the reception area. "Mr. Martin, how are you?"

"I'm okay," he said while standing up. "I just needed to talk with you."

"Okay," Patty said as she motioned with her hand for him to follow her. "There's a room down the hall we can use. Detective Starker's already there."

Patty sat next to Rick at the six-by-four-foot table with their backs to the two-way mirror while Spencer Martin sat on the opposite side with his back against the wall. Patty started the conversation. "Thanks for coming in, Mr. Martin. On the phone you said that you've remembered telling someone that your sister kept her life savings under her mattress. Is that why you're here?"

"Yeah," he replied.

Patty waited for more information, and when none was forthcoming, she asked, "Please tell us the name of the person and how you know him."

Mr. Martin looked down at the floor while holding his hands together tightly. "Well, this is terrible. I mean I can't believe that he would've killed Lola for the money. If he did, I'll never forgive myself."

Patty and Rick glanced at each other, and Patty nodded. Rick looked at the man now wringing his hands. "Who, Mr. Martin? What's his name?"

Spencer Martin looked at Rick. "Marzi," he said.

"Is that his first or last name?" Rick asked.

Lola's brother moved his head back and forth. "I don't know," he said. "Just Marzi. It's the only name he gave me and the only one I heard him called."

"And how do you know this Marzi?" Rick asked.

"Well, he lived next door to me at one time, and we'd smoke a little weed now and then. He moved about a year ago but came around a few times, and we'd smoke a little and talk."

"Why'd you tell him about your sister?" Rick asked.

"Well, he met her once a couple years ago and would ask me how she was doing every time he'd come over. The last time I saw him he was asking about her and asked me if I'd invite her over to smoke with us. I told him she wasn't interested in pot and wasn't his type. I said that she was a responsible person."

Rick and Patty exchanged glances. "And then what?" Patty asked. "What did you say to him about Lola's money?"

"Marzi said maybe I didn't really know what Lola liked and that he could take good care of her if she'd let him." Mr. Martin looked up at Patty and then Rick. "I told him Lola didn't need anyone to take care of her because she had her own money. And that's when, I think, I told him she's been saving for years under her mattress."

"What does this Marzi look like?" Rick asked.

Spencer slumped in his chair and stared at the floor. "He's got shoulder-length black hair, a beard, and is a little taller than me, so maybe five foot eleven. He's a skinny guy and looks pretty messed up most of the time. Oh, and one of his eyes is sort of half closed. Like something he was born with.

You know, I knew he stole stuff, but I never thought of him as someone who would kill somebody."

Rick asked, "When's the last time you saw this guy?"

"Just before Lola was killed. He came by my place and that's when I told him about her savings." Mr. Martin looked up at Patty and Rick. "Did I get my sister killed?"

"We don't know," Patty said. "Where does he live?"

Spencer shook his head. "I don't think he ever mentioned where he moved to. I do know that he has friends in Curry County, and I think he mentioned once driving down to Harbor, but I don't know where any of them live."

"What kind of a car does he drive?" Rick asked.

Mr. Martin turned his head to the side, closed his eyes, and furrowed his brows as though he were deep in thought. "It's a two-door. I'm pretty sure it's a Honda Civic or something like that. It has some paint missing where it was sideswiped by another car."

"Do you have a phone number for him?" Rick asked.

"No. We never spoke on the phone. He'd just drop in."

"Okay, Mr. Martin," Patty said. "You call us right away if you hear from Marzi."

Spencer Martin stood up. "I hope it wasn't him. I hope I didn't cause Lola's death."

Rick and Patty walked around the desk and Patty showed Mr. Martin back to the reception area. "We'll be in touch," she said.

"Sure," he said as Patty turned to walk back to her office where she paused and spoke to Rick. "I'm going down the hall to bring the LT current on our cases."

"Okay," Rick said. "I'll make the calls we discussed."

Patty found the lieutenant's door open. "Come on in O'Toole," he said.

Patty stepped into the office. "Thanks, LT. We've got a tentative match on footprints for the Pistol River burglary, the Havens, and our deceased couple. I've also come to realize that the burglaries in Pistol River and at the home of the elderly couple both happened on a Sunday. The Havens were gone three days, so the suspects could have broken in on Friday, Saturday, or Sunday."

The lieutenant continued to listen, and Patty went on. "I'm wondering if the victims all attend the same church service on Sunday, and if the time of that service is known by the suspects."

"That's good thinking," said the lieutenant.

"Rick's making calls now."

The lieutenant nodded. "We know the type of knot that was used to tie up the old couple, and the caliber of gun that was used to kill them. Do you know if anyone's submitting a ViCAP report?"

"I don't, but I'll find out," Patty said, "and send one in if it hasn't been done yet."

"What are your thoughts on the double homicide and the murder of Lola Martin being the same suspect?"

"Rick and I have discussed the differences between the two cases and we don't think they're related. Whoever killed Lola Martin seemed to do so suddenly and then, possibly, had a little remorse since he carefully laid her out on the bed. We expect there was only one responsible. It was most likely two robbers involved in the killing of the elderly couple, and I expect that one or both could be a sociopath."

The lieutenant sat silent for a few seconds. "I tend to agree with you, O'Toole. Find out what all was stolen and check all the pawnshops between Crescent City and Bandon. Make sure to let Josephine, Jackson, Coos, and Del Norte counties know about the robbery. These guys will most likely kill again. The sheriff is on the Major Crimes Team for this. Ask if he can arrange to have the information disseminated to sheriff's offices in each of those counties."

"The sheriff's already done that. I'll talk with him again tomorrow morning. There have been a rash of burglaries lately, and maybe he's found a connection."

"That's great," said the lieutenant before pausing. "One other thing. The elderly couple was tied up. Make sure that the knots are photographed and preserved. Check, too, for tool marks left on the damaged slider door lock."

"Okay."

"What about the Lola Martin case?" the lieutenant asked. "You talk with the brother?"

"We just did, LT, and the brother gave us the name of a guy he talked to about his sister's cash stashed under the mattress. He said the guy's name is Marzi. Doesn't know if that's a first or last name. Just Marzi."

"The brother give you a description?" asked the lieutenant.

"He did," Patty said. "And this Marzi has one lazy eye that is permanently half closed. Shouldn't be hard to ID if we can find him. Rick's going to talk to an informant we've used in the past. See if the guy might be in Harbor."

"Anything else?" asked the lieutenant.

"No. Not now."

"Good work, O'Toole. Keep me informed."

Patty nodded as she stood up and turned toward the door. "Will do."

The lieutenant stood up and walked over to see his detective out the door. "You and Rick be careful out there. You may come across the responsibles by surprise as you work deeper into these cases."

Patty nodded as she left the room and walked back down the hall. Rick was just hanging up his phone when Patty returned to her desk. "I'll call Dan Jones. Find out if he knows whether a ViCAP report was filed on the elderly couple's death."

Rick nodded. "If you reach him at the Harbor substation, you might want to check in with PO Heart or Larsen and ask if this guy Marzi is in their system."

"Good idea," Patty said before dialing. Two rings later, Dan picked up her call. "Detective Jones."

"Hey, Dan," Patty said. "Do you have a minute?"

"Sure, Patty. This about the double homicide?"

"It is," she said. "I'm wondering if anyone has input the crime details into the FBI ViCAP system?"

"I did last week," he said. "It was my first time using the system since a training I attended six months ago. I didn't know until the training that ViCAP is the only national law enforcement database that contains both investigative and behavioral information related to specific types of cases. It took me most of the day. The course instructor mentioned that many agencies don't use it because of the cumbersome amount of reporting involved. With our current situation, I wish this wasn't the case."

Patty agreed. "We just have to hope that if these suspects have committed similar crimes elsewhere, they were investigated by an agency that uses the system. I went through the program about eight years ago and have used it a couple of times. The Canadians have a similar program that has proved to be quite successful. They've given it a slightly different name than our Violent Criminal Apprehension Program, but the mission is the same."

"Share information to help solve serial crimes," Dan said.

"Yep," Patty said. "I'm sure you learned the history. The system was developed more than thirty years ago and stemmed from the belief that criminals' methods were unique enough to serve as a kind of behavioral DNA, allowing identification based upon how a person acted rather than genetic make-up."

"Just talking," Dan said, "about how effective it can be in solving serial crimes makes it difficult to understand why every agency isn't taking the time to use it."

"I agree," Patty said. "Have you received any feedback since inputting information on the double homicide?"

"Nothing yet," Dan said, "but I'll let you know if I do. It's hard for me to believe that the responsibles haven't murdered before, given the manner in which they were so cold-blooded with the one here."

"It would seem that way," Patty said. "Thanks."

Rick heard Patty's side of the conversation and waited to get back to his work until she was off the phone.

After ending the call, Patty made a few notes in the file and looked up at Rick. "Dan said that he filed a ViCAP report last week and hasn't heard anything yet."

"I heard what you said to him about the system. I trained on it a couple decades ago in Boston, where our investigations routinely fell into the cases that meet ViCAP criteria. Crimes like homicides, attempted homicides, sexual assaults, missing persons, and unidentified human remains. I heard you mention the lack of use being due to the length of time it takes inputting all of the information. From what I've read, it's also due to the lack of FBI analysts who know how to monitor the database from their offices in Virginia."

"It's a shame," Patty said. "Let's hope it comes through with something for us."

# CHAPTER 12

"**W**hat did Dan say when you asked if a PO is in?" Rick asked. "I'd like to find out if either of them knows this Marzi guy."

"PO Heart is in," Patty said. "See if she knows the guy. When you're done, let's make a few calls and find out whether any of our burglary victims attend church regularly. You want to take the elderly couple and I'll take the Havens and the Pistol River victims?"

Rick nodded and proceeded to call PO Heart.

Patty picked up a file from the stack on her desk and opened it to the first page, locating the phone number for the Havens. "Hello Mrs. Haven. This is Detective O'Toole. Do you have a few minutes to talk?"

"Oh sure, Detective." Patty could hear a muffled voice repeating her name and figured Mrs. Haven must have her hand over the phone receiver while letting her husband know who was on the phone. "Did you find the burglars?" she asked Patty.

"Not yet, Mrs. Haven, but we're working on it. I have a couple of questions to ask."

"Oh, of course," she said sounding a little disappointed. "What do you need to know?"

"Do you and Mr. Haven attend church regularly?"

"Why, yes we do," she said. "That is whenever we're in town we do. Sometimes when we're travelling we don't find a church near enough for us to attend Sunday service. Why do you ask?"

"It's just a theory I'm working on," Patty said before continuing. "What church do you attend and on what day of the week?"

"We attend the Hope Christian Church on Sunday mornings, Detective. Always the eleven o'clock service."

"Thank you," Patty replied. "Tell me, Mrs. Haven. Are there any regular events at the church that you might attend?"

"Well, let me think. There are a lot of events at the church, but the one we probably go to every year is the Thanksgiving gathering. It's a wonderful dinner and garage sale."

"Okay," Patty said. "I'll be in touch if I have any more questions. Thanks for your time."

"No need to thank us, Detective. We hope you catch the guys who took my jewelry and Dick's gun."

"We appreciate your help. Goodbye," Patty said.

Rick was still on the phone when Patty made a few notes in the Havens' file and picked up the file for the Pistol River burglary victims. As she reached for the receiver, she heard Officer Bradley call in for her over the radio. She picked up her portable and said, "go ahead."

"We're on our way as back up to the sheriff's unit. A reserve deputy was down at the harbor and spotted our suspect, Marzi, on a bike. Said the bike rider looked like the photo we distributed this morning. A man claiming to be the owner of the bike rode it down to the harbor. He left his bike out front of the convenience store for a couple of minutes while he stopped in to buy a coke. When he exited the store, he saw some guy riding off with his bike."

"Copy that," Patty said. "The bike owner say anything about the suspect?"

"Affirmative," Brad said. "Says he saw the guy standing outside the store before he went in. His description of what the suspect is wearing matches what the reserve gave me: blue jeans, a black t-shirt, and shoulder-length hair. The bike owner was able to add one extra detail."

"What's that?" Patty asked.

"He said the guy has one eye that looked to be half closed."

"Sounds like our guy, Brad. We'll drive down Benham Lane. If he sees you and feels blocked in, he may have to exit up the hill from Lower Harbor Road."

"Which means he'll have to walk his bike," Brad said.

"And that will slow him down a bit," Patty said as she stood up and signaled to Rick that they needed to leave. "We're leaving now," she said to Brad.

Patty explained the call to Rick as he started up their unmarked car and turned on the grill-mounted lights to clear traffic. "I figure it'll take him at least ten minutes to Benham considering he'll have to walk up the hill," Patty said.

The radio crackled and Brad came on. "No sign of him here at the harbor, so we're driving up to Benham. Why don't you turn onto Oceanview on the chance he's got friends at one of the storage units."

"Will do," Rick replied. "We're just about there now."

Rick and Patty arrived at the turnoff on Oceanview just as they could see Brad and Chekowsky coming up the hill.

"There he is," Patty said to Rick and then raised Brad on the radio. "He's in front of us and knows we're onto him. I expect he'll soon ditch the bike and take off on foot. If that happens, we may need more officers."

"Dispatch, did you copy that? We'll need additional units," Brad said.

The suspect did as expected, ditched the bike and started running as Rick and Patty drove up behind him. Rick put the car in park and started running after the suspect while Patty got back on the radio to Brad. "The suspect is running across the properties toward Pedrioli. We need someone to come down that way from the highway." Patty then got into the driver's seat, started the car, and drove to Pedrioli, where she turned toward the highway. She drove up a short way and could see the suspect running in her direction. Patty left the vehicle and started off between the homes after the suspect. When the suspect saw her, he stopped momentarily and looked around, seeing Rick quickly closing in on him. As he began running again, this time toward the highway, he saw two officers running toward him."

Patty called out, "Police! Stop!" She could see that the suspect realized he had no possible chance of getting away and stood looking toward Patty. "Get on the ground with your hands out to your sides!" she yelled. When the suspect didn't move right away, Patty yelled out again. "Now! On the ground with your hands out to your sides!" This time the suspect did as he was instructed.

Rick ran up, out of breath and irritated that the suspect didn't surrender earlier in the run. He pulled out his handcuffs, cuffed the suspect's hands behind him, and helped him up to his feet.

"I just borrowed the bike," said the suspect. "There's no reason for you to arrest me. I'll take it back to the store."

"Well, Mr. Marzi," Patty said. This got the attention of the suspect as Patty continued. "It is Marzi, right? We've got a few questions to ask you."

Rick walked the suspect back to where Brad had parked his car. They put him in the caged backseat of the marked car and asked that Brad transport the prisoner to the B.P.D. As they rode back to the station, Patty spoke to Rick. "That was quite a workout. I didn't know you could run like that."

"I didn't either," Rick said. "And it's made me really hungry. Let Mr. Marzi sit and worry in lockup while we go eat lunch."

After eating, the detectives drove back to their office where they had the suspect brought into an interview room. He was seated facing the two-way mirror and handcuffed to a large metal ring secured to the table. Before going into the room Patty said to Rick. "I'll be good cop to your bad."

"So what's new?" Rick asked.

When the detectives entered, Rick sat down in front of the suspect while Patty stood off to the side.

"What's your name?" Rick asked.

"You know my name. You called me Marzi."

Rick leaned forward toward the suspect. "What's your full name?"

The suspect looked around the room, gazing for a couple of seconds up and to the right. "I don't have another name," he said. "Just call me Marzi."

"Well, Marzi," Rick said. "Detective O'Toole and I brought you down here just to ask a few questions, but it seems you're going to be a problem. That right, Marzi? You going to be a problem?"

Marzi squirmed a bit in his seat. "Look," he said. "I just took that bike because I wanted to visit a friend. You've got the bike back now, so why not just let me go?"

"Well, sir," Patty said, "we have some questions for you, but I'd first like to read your rights." Patty pulled out her Miranda card and read through it for the prisoner. She then asked, "Do you understand each of these rights I've explained to you?" Patty then waited for the suspect to respond before going on.

"Yeah," he said.

"Having these rights in mind, do you wish to talk to us now?"

The prisoner hesitated. "What happens if I don't want to answer your questions?"

Patty started to stand up to leave. "We'll have you taken to jail where you'll sit while we get a court date set."

"Okay," Marzi said. "I agree. Go ahead and ask your questions."

"Where'd you get the bike?" Patty asked.

"Well, you know. I took it."

"From where did you take it?"

"From in front of the store down at the harbor. Some guy went into the store and left his bike out front."

"Was the bike locked when you took it?"

"No," he said.

"Thank you, Marzi," Patty said. "Just a few more questions."

Rick now took the lead. "Where'd you get the two hundred dollars we found in your pocket?"

Marzi leaned back in his chair, looking left and then up and to the right, again, body language suggesting he was probably creating a lie. "I won it at a poker game," he said.

"Where?" Rick asked.

"Where what?"

"Where was the poker game?" Rick asked.

"Well, it was, uhh, at some house I was at last night."

"Whose house?" Rick asked. "Where was it?"

The suspect laughed. "I don't know whose house it was, and I don't know where it was. It was dark when some guy gave me a ride there."

Rick pounded the palm of his hand down on the table. "You'd better start taking this conversation seriously, Mr. Marzi, or you're apt to find yourself spending more than just a few hours in jail."

Patty's cell phone buzzed and she looked at caller ID. She nodded to Rick and then stepped out of the room. Once outside the door, Patty answered the call, thanked the caller, and stepped back into the interview room.

"Mr. Marzelli," Patty said in a quiet tone as she walked toward the table.

The suspect looked up at Patty with concern on his face. "That call I just took was from PO Heart, and it seems you failed your last UA test and then didn't come in as you were mandated to do. Now with your stealing the bike, well, you're in big trouble." Patty looked up at Rick. "He's not interested in helping us out, so we might as well just take him to the county jail for the next couple of weeks and let him go to trial."

The suspect leaned forward in his chair. "Help you out?" he said. "Okay, look. My name is Mario Marzelli and I'm trying to stay clean. What questions do you want to ask me? If I answer your questions will you let me go?"

Patty took the lead. "Well, Mr. Marzelli, let's start by your telling us where you got the two hundred dollars you had in your pocket when we picked you up?"

Marzelli looked at Rick and then toward Patty. He then looked down at the floor. "Okay, I didn't really win it playing poker. I found it on some homeless guy sleeping under a tree along the highway."

"A homeless guy?" Patty asked. "How did you know he had it on him?"

The suspect stuttered as he responded. "How did I know he had it? Well, someone told me."

Patty continued. "Who told you?"

The suspect sat back and exhaled loudly. "I don't remember. I guess it was . . ." There was a long pause. "Well, I can't remember who told me. What difference does it make? You can have the money. Just ask your questions so that I can go."

"What kind of a car do you own?" Patty asked.

"Car? If I owned a car I wouldn't have stolen the bike."

Patty continued. "How did you get from Reedsport to here if you don't own a car?"

"I had a Honda," the suspect said. "It was stolen a few days ago."

"Stolen?" Rick asked. "Why didn't you report it?"

"I knew I'd test for meth and that I'd go back to jail if I came in."

Now Patty asked the question. "What were you doing in Reedsport?"

"Reedsport," the suspect repeated. "Why would I be in Reedsport?"

Patty could sense that they were getting close. "I asked you how you got here from Reedsport if you didn't own a car, and you told us you had a Honda. So what were you doing in Reedsport? Do you live there?"

"Uh, no," he said. "I, uh, was visiting friends."

Rick sat down next to Patty. "What friends?" he asked. "What are their names?"

The suspect now began to look concerned. "Just friends I get together with," he said.

"Friends, you get together with to smoke a little weed?" Rick asked. "Is that what you and your friends do? Friends like Spencer Martin?"

The suspect was now visibly shaken. "I don't know a Spencer Martin," he said.

"Well that's odd," Rick replied. "Because Spencer Martin says he knows you. He's told us all about you. How'd you get the two hundred dollars, Mr. Marzelli?"

The suspect was now looking back and forth between Rick and Patty.

"I don't know what Spencer told you, but I found the money. I found it! I don't want to answer any more questions, and you can't make me."

The two detectives got up, left the suspect, and walked back to their office, where Patty sat down and proceeded to tap her pencil on the desk. "We've got enough to hold him on the theft but not for the murder."

Rick's cell phone rang. He looked at the caller ID and then at Patty. "This is my informant calling. Might be he has the break we need."

# CHAPTER 13

Patty saw Rick write down something on his notepad. "Thanks," he said. Then he directed his attention to Patty. "I've got a name and address of someone who knows Marzi recently came into a lot of money."

"Let's go," Patty said. "And after we check out this lead, I want to go over what we learned about the church habits of our burglary victims."

The detectives drove to the storage facility, where several people were sitting around with a bay door open. Three men and a woman were sitting in chairs, one with a sleeping bag wrapped around his shoulders. Patty and Rick walked up to the opening. "Good afternoon. I'm Detective O'Toole, and this is Detective Starker." Before she could go on, one of the three guys hollered out, "If you're here to arrest us, forget it! We pay rent for this space."

Patty responded, "We're not here to arrest anyone. Which one of you is Willie Schwartz?"

The four tenants looked at each other, and then the one with the sleeping bag spoke up. "I'm Willie," he said.

"Mr. Schwartz," Patty said, "we'd like to ask you a few questions in private. Would you mind stepping away from the storage unit?"

Willie looked at each of the other tenants and then back to the detectives. "What's this about?" he asked.

"We've just got a few questions and would rather ask you privately," Patty said.

Willie stood up and walked with the detectives back toward their car. "Sure," he said. "I'm always happy to help the police." After walking far enough away from the others so as not to be heard, Rick took the photo of Marzi out of his pocket and showed it to Willie. "Do you know this guy?"

"Yeah," he said. "That's Marzi."

Patty then spoke. "We understand Marzi recently came into quite a bit of money. What can you tell us about that?"

"What makes you think I know anything about that?" he asked.

Rick crossed his arms over his chest. "A little bird told us you were talking about Marzi and all his money. Did you help him get it?"

"No. I didn't have anything to do with it. He saw me on my bike the other day and asked if I wanted to smoke some pot with him."

"I asked him how he got the pot. I know he doesn't have a job and he's only been back here for a few days."

"What did he tell you?" Patty asked.

"Said it was a secret and that he couldn't tell me. He said he'd come into a lot of money and had it hidden."

"You said he'd only been here a few days," Rick said. "Where did he come from?"

"Reedsport," Willie said. "He told me he'd seen a couple guys I know."

"What guys?" asked Patty.

"Mike somebody and Spencer Martin," Willie said.

"Do you know Spencer Martin?" Rick asked.

"Yeah, I've known Spencer since we were kids. I don't know why he hangs out with a lowlife like Marzi."

"Why do you say that?" Patty asked.

"Well, Spencer's a pretty nice guy and Marzi, well, Marzi's a loser."

"Did Marzi say whether Spencer knew about the money?" Patty asked.

Willie looked away from the detectives. "Well, I think he said that Spencer told him about the money. I didn't pay much attention to that, though, 'cuz if Spencer knew about the money, why didn't he go after it?"

"Did Marzi mention anything about Spencer having a sister?"

"Oh yeah. Said she was the girl of his dreams. I didn't think much of that either 'cuz Marzi's always been a big talker about girls. Truth is, most of the women we know don't want to have anything to do with him."

"Willie," Patty said, "I need for you to think carefully about this before answering. Are you sure Marzi said that Spencer's sister *was* the girl of his dreams? Is it possible he said that she *is* the girl of his dreams?"

"Well, no. He said she was, because he told me she was dead."

"Willie," Patty said. "We need you to come with us to the station so that you can write out what you've told us. We'll buy you some lunch and bring you back here when we're done."

Willie rolled his eyes and looked back at his friends. "Okay," he said. "Let me tell them I'll be back in a while."

At the office Willie wrote out a statement about the part of his conversation when Marzi told him that Lola was dead. He handed the tablet back to Patty.

"This is good, Willie." Patty said. "We have just a few more questions."

"Did you already know Spencer's sister was dead when Marzi told you?"

"No, and it was kind of a shock. I mean, she didn't hang out with us, and Spencer told me she didn't smoke pot or drink. I've heard from a few other people that she'd died, but that was a couple days after Marzi told me."

"Do you remember what day it was when Marzi told you about the money and Spencer's sister being dead?"

"Well," Willie started, "my memory's not very good." Rick and Patty remained quiet while Willie thought about their questions. "Well, I guess I do remember something," he said. "I think it was on a Sunday or Monday."

Patty looked at Rick. "Sunday was the tenth," she said. "The day before Karen Gains asked that someone check in on Lola."

"Thanks, Willie. We need for you to just write that down and then we'll take you back to your friends. We'll probably need for you to answer these questions again."

"What about my lunch?" Willie asked.

Rick responded. "We'll run through McDonalds and you can order what you want."

Willie smiled as he wrote down what Marzi had told him, and when.

Patty and Rick dropped Willie off with his lunch at the storage facility and then drove back to their office.

"I need to let the LT know what we've got and then let's discuss the church habits of our double homicide victims," Patty said.

Rick nodded. "Go ahead. I still need to make a couple calls."

In the lieutenant's office, Patty explained what they'd learned. "He's written down that he thinks Marzi talked to him on either the day before we found Lola Martin, or on the same day. During their conversation Marzi told Willie that Lola was dead. Marzi also mentioned learning from Lola's brother about a large amount of money. Do you think we have enough to arrest him for Lola's murder?"

The lieutenant sat back in his chair. "First," he said, "that's good work on the part of you and Rick. Do you have enough to charge Marzi with murder? No, I don't think so."

"You don't?" Patty asked. "We've got a witness who will swear to having spoken to Marzi on, possibly, the day after she died, and being told that she was dead. We also have Marzi with a substantial amount of cash."

"You're welcome to talk with the DA about it, O'Toole," said the LT. "But I don't think you have enough. You don't know that the cash Spencer told Marzi about is the same money that you found on Marzi. You need to prove that Marzi was in Lola's house on the day she died." The lieutenant could see Patty's frustration as she faced the fact that she and Rick didn't have enough evidence. "Let's say Marzi did take Lola's money," he said. "What else was in that house that Marzi may have taken? What else did Lola Martin have that would have been of value to Marzi?"

Patty paused, looking down at the floor, and then looked back at the lieutenant. "Her gun," she said. "Lola's brother said that at one time she told him she had a gun. There was no gun found when her house was searched. I'll check the records and find out if she purchased one within the past few years."

The lieutenant nodded in agreement. "You and Rick find her gun, and someone who can swear to having received it from Marzi, and you'll have enough."

Patty got up, and on her way out of the office, turned back to the lieutenant. "Thanks LT," she said.

"You're welcome, O'Toole. When is your next meeting with the Major Crimes Team?"

"Tomorrow," Patty said. "I'll let you know if we come up with anything new."

"Okay," said the lieutenant.

Back at her desk, Patty shared with Rick the conversation she'd had with their lieutenant. "It won't be difficult to find out if she bought a gun within the past several years. But finding the gun won't be so easy. Do you think your informant can help us out again?"

"I'll find out," Rick said. "Did you want to go over the church information on the other case now?"

"Yeah, I do. I've spoken with the Havens, but I had to leave a message for the Bensons in Pistol River. Give me a minute and I'll try them, again, now."

"Sure," Rick said. "I'm going to check with OSP for any firearms purchased by Lola Martin."

After three rings a woman answered Patty's call. "Hello Mrs. Benson," Patty said. "This is Detective O'Toole with the Brookings Police Department. I'm working with the Major Crimes Team toward finding the person or persons who broke into your home."

"Hello Detective," she replied. "Deputy Kindle said we might receive a call from you. Have you found the person responsible for our burglary?"

"Not yet, Mrs. Benson, but we're getting closer. I'm calling to ask if you regularly attend a local church service?"

"Well, yes we do. We like the Hope Christian Church in Brookings. It's a bit of a drive for us, but we enjoy it because of the scenery. Why do you ask? Do you think someone we know from church broke into our home?"

"We don't know that someone from your church had anything to do with the burglary, but we're checking on all leads. Your church also has a Thanksgiving dinner and garage sale. Is that something you and Mr. Benson attend?"

"We used to, but we've been gone for the past couple of years during the time of that dinner."

"That's helpful information, Mrs. Benson. Is there anything you can tell me about people who work at the church? Is it always the same people helping out?"

"Let me think," she said. "We have volunteers who, I think, change every week for some of the tasks. There are a few paid individuals, including our pastor, the janitor, and Miriam, who works in the office."

"What kind of tasks do the volunteers do?" Patty asked.

"Well, you should probably asked Miriam about that. She's the one who schedules everyone."

"Okay, Mrs. Benson. I'll do that. Thank you for your time."

"No problem, Detective. I hope you find my jewelry and my husband's gun."

"We hope so, too, Mrs. Benson. Good bye."

Rick was off the phone and waited for Patty to end her call. "Two years ago Lola Martin purchased a Glock 19," he said.

"I'll bet it's still here in the county," Patty said. "Marzi gave it away or sold it to someone. We just need to figure out who."

Patty then picked up her notepad. "Seems we have a church in common with both the Havens and the Bensons. Both couples attend the Hope Christian Church here in Brookings every Sunday that they're in town. Were you able to find out about our homicide victims?"

"According to the neighbors," Rick said, "they, too, attended the Hope Christian Church. I think you may have hit on something, Patty."

"Okay," Patty said. "Let's drive over to the church and find out what we can about the people who volunteer and work there."

"I'll be right with you," Rick said as he stepped out of the office. A minute later he came back in with a couple of cookies. Looking at Patty he said, "There's more in the break room if you're interested. One of our volunteers brought them in."

"I'll pass," she said. "I'm just eager, now, to talk with the church secretary. Let's go."

Rick drove them the three miles to the church, where he and Patty parked and then walked up to a door at the building entrance. They found the door unlocked and walked into an entrance hall. The door was open to a small office where they saw an elderly woman sitting at the desk reading. "May I help you?" she asked.

"I hope so," Patty said showing her badge to the woman. "We're Detectives O'Toole and Starker. We're investigating a crime, and we'd like to talk with you a few minutes. Is this convenient for you?"

"Oh sure, Detectives. It's pretty quiet here at this time of day. What can I help you with?"

"How many employees does the church have?" Patty asked.

"We have four. We have a janitor, a gardener, the pastor, of course, and then me."

"Thank you," Patty said. "How often are the janitor and gardener here?"

The secretary opened her drawer and pulled out a file. "I have their hours here in my file. Let me see," she said as she thumbed through a couple pages. "Our gardener is here every Friday for as long as it takes to cut the grass and trim the bushes. The janitor comes only once a week, too. He's here every Monday between eight and noon."

Rick was taking notes as Patty continued to ask questions. "What about volunteers. When do you use volunteers?"

The secretary turned another page in the file. "We use volunteers every Sunday and for special events. On Sundays they welcome people into the church and help the pastor during the service. Oh, and we generally have a volunteer out front helping direct people with their parking."

Patty looked up at Rick and then back to the secretary. "Do you have the same people volunteering every Sunday?"

"Pretty much," she said. "You know how it is trying to get people to volunteer. The guy who helps with the parking is our newest volunteer, and he's been coming every Sunday for the past three months."

Patty looked to the file. "What's his name?"

"Jim Severs," said the secretary. "I hope he's not in trouble again."

"In trouble *again?*" Patty asked.

"Yes. He's one of the guys our pastor has helped. Jim was homeless when our pastor first met him and brought him to the church. Jim told Pastor that he'd been in jail before for stealing. He promised he wouldn't steal again if Pastor could help him. So one of our parishioners agreed to let Jim use their extra bedroom and share meals with them. That came to an end last month, though, when those parishioners moved. I don't know what Jim's been doing about a place to stay. Looking at his sign-in sheet, it appears he continued to help out with Sunday parking until recently."

"So you haven't seen him in three weeks?" Patty asked.

"No, we haven't," she said.

Rick looked at his notes and then to the secretary. "How did Mr. Severs get here? Does he have a car or a bike?"

"Well, I'm pretty sure he doesn't have a car, and I'm not sure about a bike. The parishioners he was living with used to bring him to the church with them."

"Do you think your pastor might know?" Rick asked.

"Yes, he might," she said. "He'll be back in an hour. I'll ask him about it then."

Patty stood up. "We'd appreciate that. Ask him, too, if he's seen Mr. Severs in the past couple of weeks, or if he knows where the man might be staying." Patty handed her card to the woman. "Please call me with his answers."

"Okay, Detective. It'll be this afternoon."

"Thank you," Patty said as she and Rick left.

# CHAPTER 14

Back at their office, Rick and Patty went over what they'd learned. "We've got three couples who all attended the same church service," Rick said. "And a church volunteer who would have seen all three couples, knew their church attendance patterns and their cars.

"Let's run Jim Severs' name through the system. Find out what we can," Patty said. "I'm wondering why these three couples and not others?"

"What do you mean?" Rick asked.

"I mean, why were these three targeted? And are there others who've already been targeted and just not burglarized yet?"

"Maybe we'll find answers talking again with the Havens and Bensons. They may have spoken with Severs."

"We should do that now," Patty said. "I just spoke with Mrs. Benson, so I'll call her back. You call the Havens and see what you can find."

Mrs. Benson answered Patty's call. "Hello detective," she said. "You must have more questions."

"I do, Mrs. Benson. We've learned that there's a volunteer at the church who helps with parking on Sundays. Do you know who I mean?"

"Oh, sure. That's Jim. He's a nice guy that the pastor met and invited to help out with the parking. We thank him for his help when we see him."

"In your conversations with Jim, Mrs. Benson, has he ever asked you where you live? This is important, so please think carefully."

"Not that I recall," she said. "Most of our conversation has just been thanking him for helping us with parking, and his thanking us for the small tips we give him."

"Tips?" Patty asked. "Do you mean that you pay him?"

"Yes, not a lot, but the tips some of us give help him to stay out of the shelters. Especially since the people moved who had given him a place to sleep and eat."

"How do you pay him, Mrs. Benson? Do you give him cash?"

"Oh no," she said. "The pastor asked that if we wanted to help Jim out, we could give the money to the church secretary, who could then help Jim learn how to maintain a bank account and keep track of his bills. She must have told Jim who made the donations because we'd always get a 'thank you' if we saw him in the parking lot."

"And how did you make the payment?" Patty asked.

"With a check," said Mrs. Benson.

"Do your checks have your home address on them?"

"Well, yes they do, Detective. You don't think? Oh my. I just can't believe that Jim would do anything to harm us after our being so kind to him. Do you?"

"I don't know, Mrs. Benson," Patty said. "We'll be in touch."

When Patty hung up the phone, Rick was still on the call with the Havens. He looked up at Patty, who wrote on a tablet that she then put in front of Rick. Rick read it and then asked the question of Mrs. Haven.

"Mrs. Haven, have you ever given Jim, the man who helps find parking for you, a tip?"

"Yes we have, Detective. We've written a couple of checks that we've given to the church secretary for Jim." Rick confirmed that the Havens' home address was on their checks.

Patty called the church secretary back, asking for additional information. "How did Jim Severs know who was making the donations he received?"

"Oh," she said. "I thought it was important he be able to thank the donors, so I make copies of the checks for him."

"We'll need the name and contact information for every parishioner who had written Jim Severs a check since he first started volunteering at the church," Patty said.

Patty gave Rick the information she'd received from the church secretary. "We've got a Major Crimes Team meeting in Gold Beach tomorrow morning, and we'll have to leave early. There's not much more we can do today, so I'll see you in the morning about seven."

"I'm out of here, too," Rick said as he put his files away.

# CHAPTER 15

The following morning Patty and Rick drove to the sheriff's office in Gold Beach for the Major Crime Team meeting and met with the sheriff, Detective Dan Jones, Deputy Ted Kindle, and OSP Trooper Jackson.

"Thanks for the doughnuts," the sheriff said as Rick set down a large pastry box in the middle of the table. "Coffee's in the break room."

Everyone was seated with coffee cup in hand when each agency exchanged with each other copies of their reports to date.

Patty started the conversation. "Rick and I were given information yesterday that leads us to believe the victims were targeted by a guy volunteering at the Hope Christian Church in Brookings."

"All three couples attended the same service at the church," Rick said. "The suspect, a guy the pastor was helping, directed church attendees toward available parking before the service. Some attendees, including the victims in all three burglarized homes, thanked the suspect by giving personal checks to the church secretary, made payable to the suspect."

Patty continued the reporting. "The secretary then gave copies of the checks to the suspect so that he'd know who was helping him. Victims in all three residences have their home addresses on the checks they used."

"Well," said Ted, "that gave the responsibles all they needed. Did you get the guy's name?"

"Jim Severs," Rick said. "He's in the system for burglary a couple years ago. Pretty quiet since then. He was living on the street until one of the pastor's parishioners took him in for a period of time. The people who took him in moved about three weeks ago."

"Do you know where he is now?" the sheriff asked.

"We don't," said Patty. "He recently quit showing up at the church." Patty directed her next questions to the state trooper. "Do you have an answer yet on the footprints?"

"No. The state crime lab is so backed up that it could be months before we hear anything. Our best bet might be with the lead you have on the parking attendant." Before he could go on, text messages making a cacophony of tones came up on each of their cell phones. "It's a response from ViCAP," he said.

"The system found similarities in the rope knots," Patty said with excitement.

Rick, with equal excitement said, "Federal Way, Washington, input their double homicide into the system. It's the same M.O. The couple was tied up with a rope and each was shot twice in the chest."

"With the same suspects responsible for homicides in two states, I'll contact the FBI, let them know what we've got, and find out if they have any interest in this," said the sheriff.

"I'll talk with Federal Way," Patty said, "and Rick and I will put out an all-points bulletin on Jim Severs."

"Do you have a photo of Severs?" asked the trooper.

Rick nodded. "We were able to get one from the church pastor. He's standing with a group of parishioners, so it's only a head shot, but it's straight on and clear."

The sheriff closed his binder. "That's all we've got here. Let's meet again in a couple of days unless we need to do so sooner."

Rick took a second doughnut out of the box, and he and Patty walked out to their car. "I'll wait until we're back at the office to call Federal Way," she said. "No sense having the call drop several times between here and there."

"These are some pretty cold-blooded killers," Rick said.

*     *     *

After returning to their office, Patty sat down at her desk and pulled out her notepad as Rick walked to his desk with a fresh cup of coffee. "Let's go over what we've got before I call Federal Way," she said.

"Sure," said Rick. "We've got two home burglaries, one of which we know for certain occurred while the residents were attending the eleven o'clock church service at the Hope Christian Church. We expect the Havens, who regularly attended the same service, were also burglarized the same Sunday morning."

Patty continued the list. "Victims of the double homicide were gone three days but the ME puts their death within the same time as the church service attended by the other two couples. We've got footprint casts from two of the three residences that appear to be the same print, though we don't yet have scientific confirmation. The homicide victims each died with two shots to the chest."

"And," said Rick, "I found a cartridge on the floor, fired from a 9-mm striker-fired pistol."

"Patty continued to review the list. "Jewelry was taken from all three residences, guns from two of the three homes, and possibly codeine from the home of the homicide victims."

Rick finished writing and said, "And we now have the probable M.O. of the suspects, using a church parking attendant to acquire address information."

Patty picked up the phone receiver. "I need to give what we have to Federal Way and find out if it fits their case."

"While you do that," Rick said, "I'll return a call to my informant. Looks like he left a message while we were in Gold Beach."

Patty called and was transferred to the Federal Way PD detective working their double homicide. Detective Sajak answered and Patty identified herself. "I've got to say," she said to the detective, "it was great to learn that you used the ViCAP system so soon after your homicide."

"Yea, it was a surprise to me, too, to get the match from Brookings. I just finished the course last month."

"Time well spent," Patty said. "So let me tell you what we've got."

After she explained the church connection to the suspects, Sajak commented, "If our suspects are operating in the same manner here, we may need to warn a list of parishioners."

"I've got an idea," Patty said. "Let me know how many addresses our suspects may have and whether you find the same type of practice by a volunteer at the church. We can then stake out each residence during next Sunday's service. Our suspects may walk right into our hands."

"That might work," said the detective. "I'll make a few calls and get back with you."

"Okay," Patty said. "Let me give you my cell phone number."

Rick waited until Patty hung up and then filled her in on his call. "My informant thinks he might know who has Lola's gun and said he needs a couple days. If he steers us right, I'll get with Crime Stoppers and see if they'll help me with a reward of some kind."

"Good idea, Rick. Your informant came through before, so let's hope he can do so again, and that we get lucky before Marzi's court date on the stolen bike."

Rick shook his head. "We sure don't want him released due to an overcrowded jail."

"Oh," Patty said, "I almost forgot. My mom called and left a message on my cell phone. She and Bill had tickets to a local play and have changed their plans. She's offering the tickets to me. I do plan to see the play, but I thought that you and Barbara could use the tickets. It's a great mystery thriller at the Chetco Pelican Players' playhouse."

"What's the Chetco, what kind of playhouse?" Rick asked, not having understood the name.

Patty lifted her eyebrows. "Haven't you ever been to a play by the Chetco Pelican Players? They're great! The playhouse is on the north side of town near O'Holleran's. Becky and I have been to many of their performances and have enjoyed them all. You'd be amazed at the high caliber of talent we have here in small-town Brookings."

"When is it?" Rick asked.

"The last performance is the Sunday after next," Patty said. "Think Barbara might want to go?"

"Well, she might want to, but she can't. She's worked every day for the past two weeks, and she's already told me that with open houses and client meetings, she's working through the next two weekends."

"Wow, she sure is busy." Patty said.

"Yeah," Rick said. "Anyway, thanks for offering."

Patty paused. "You know, I want to see the play, and Becky can't go, and you seem to be free that Sunday, so why don't we use the tickets? I mean, if you want to use the second ticket."

Rick paused, looking at Patty, and then broke into a big grin. "Are you asking me out?"

"No," Patty responded quickly. "It's not a date or anything like that. I just thought that since we both want to go, we might as well use the tickets. But no, it's not a date."

Rick continued to grin as Patty rolled her eyes.

"Okay," he said. "I'll go with you but only if you let me buy the popcorn."

Patty shook her head. "It starts at two. I'll go early and reserve a couple of seats and meet you there."

"I'll be there," Rick said still grinning.

Patty's phone rang and she quickly picked up the receiver, grateful to leave the prior conversation. "O'Toole," she answered.

# Chapter 16

"Detective O'Toole, this is Pastor Nick at the Hope Christian Church. You spoke with my secretary yesterday about a volunteer of ours."

"Yes, Nick. She told us about Jim Severs. Have you seen him since he quit helping at the church?"

"Well," he said, "it happens that I saw him yesterday. He was walking down Chetco Avenue when I came out of the credit union. I asked how he was doing."

"What did he say?" Patty asked.

"He apologized for not showing up at the church. Said something had come up and he couldn't help us out anymore."

"Did you ask him where he's living? Patty asked.

"Not exactly. I asked if he'd found someplace to live and he said 'yes.' He didn't give me an address, and I didn't ask for one."

"Do you know if he has a car or a bike?" asked Patty.

"To my knowledge, he does not."

"Okay," Patty said. "Please give me a call if you see him again."

"Detective," the pastor said. "Has Jim committed a crime? Is he in trouble again?"

"We don't know," Patty said. "A crime has been committed, and we need to talk with him."

Patty heard the pastor exhale. "Okay," he said. "I'll let you know if I see him."

Patty hung up the phone and looked over at Rick, one cookie in his hand and two more on his desk. Laughing, she said, "It's only been a couple hours since we had lunch."

Rick looked into her eyes. "And your point is?" he asked.

Patty's cell phone rang and she shook her head as she looked at the caller ID. Letting the call go to voicemail, Rick asked, "You mad at someone?"

"No," Patty said. "It's that Luke Mason. I was clear after our glass of wine that I wasn't interested in dating, but he hasn't accepted the message."

"Maybe you need to be more forceful," Rick said.

"No. He's just a very needy guy. He'll eventually get the message if I don't return his calls." Then changing the subject, Patty said, "We seem to be on the cusp of solving both of our homicide cases right now. If your informant comes through with the name of the person who has Lola's gun, it could break that case wide open."

"Yea," Rick said. "And if the M.O. on our double homicide is the same as that used in Federal Way, we could be close to closing in on those suspects." Before they could further discuss the cases, Patty's desk phone rang.

"O'Toole," she said. "Yeah, go ahead and transfer the call."

"Detective O'Toole, this is Detective Sajak from Federal Way. After talking with the daughter of our double homicide victims, and one of our local churches, it appears to be the same responsibles. We had a second burglary last Sunday. The homicide victims as well as the second home were burglarized on the same date. I didn't put it together until after our conversation this morning. The victims in both homes attend a small, local Christian church and attend the same Sunday service. The daughter of the homicide victims said her parents were home because her father was sick with a cold and flu."

"Did the church's pastor have any idea how the suspects obtained addresses of the victims?" Patty asked.

"Same as what occurred there in Brookings," said Sajak. "There was a volunteer helping out with parking at the church. He received name and address information from the secretary about the attendees who gave him tips. The pastor said that the volunteer just started showing up a few weeks ago."

"Let me talk with the others on my Major Crimes Team," Patty said. "The sheriff was going to contact the FBI. I'll talk with him and give you a call back. I think we may have an opportunity to catch our suspects in the act."

"I've got the names of others whose addresses may be known by the suspects," Sajak said. "I'll need to contact them before Sunday morning."

"I understand," Patty said. "I'd appreciate your holding off until after we've developed a plan. We're going to need help."

"I'll contact the Washington State Patrol," said Sajak. "The WSP has an Investigating Services Bureau and an Investigation Assistance Division."

"That's great," Patty said. "We're going to need them. I'll get back with you later today."

After ending her call with Detective Sajak, Patty briefed Rick on what she'd learned. "I'm going in to talk with the LT before I call others on the team."

Rick nodded as Patty left the room and walked down the hall.

"Come in, O'Toole," said the lieutenant.

"Hi, LT," Patty said. "I've got new information on both homicide cases."

"Great," he responded. "Let's start with the Martin case."

Patty proceeded to fill in the lieutenant on what she and Rick had learned. "We're waiting to hear from Rick's informant, who thinks he may know who has the gun that was purchased by our victim. We're hoping to find it before Marzi's released."

"Explain to the DA what you've got and ask that Marzi be held a few more days," said the lieutenant.

"Okay," Patty said before switching to the next case. "The PD in Federal Way, Washington has a double homicide in which a rope and knot were used that are similar to our case. Detective Sajak in Federal Way used the ViCAP system and the information was sent to all of us on the Major Crimes Team while we were at this morning's meeting in Gold Beach."

"Good to know the system works when used," said the lieutenant. "Does Federal Way have any other evidence similar to our crimes?"

"I just got off the phone with Sajak, and they had a second burglary on the same Sunday as their double homicide. In both cases the homeowners were known to attend the ten-o'clock service at their local church."

The lieutenant asked, "What about the manner in which a volunteer was used to transfer information on the addresses of our victims?"

"A few weeks ago a volunteer began showing up at their church to help out. He specifically asked to direct parking. According the their church secretary, he mentioned that he'd be grateful to anyone who'd like to tip him, and explained how he'd received tips at other churches for doing the same thing."

"What's your plan, O'Toole?"

"I've asked Sajak to hold off on alerting the other church members whose addresses may be in the hands of the responsibles, at least until I've spoken with the rest of the team. I think we should plan surveillance at the homes of the other potential victims. There's a good chance we can take the responsibles in progress."

"Do you have enough help to observe every residence?"

"Sajak is contacting the WSP Investigative Assistance Division," Patty said. "They should be able to provide us with the additional help we're going to need. The sheriff contacted the FBI, but they don't seem much interested unless we have a name for them."

"Yeah," said the lieutenant. "That seems to be the way they operate. We do the work and arrest the responsible, then the FBI will pick him up and take the credit. Seems that between your team, Sajak, and WSP, you'll be able to catch the suspects."

"I believe we will."

"Let me know if you need my help. Good work, O'Toole."

"Thanks," Patty said before walking back to her desk. "I'm thinking that we should set up a conference call with our team members," she said to Rick, "giving them the information on Federal Way. We should then set up another call on which Sajak and someone from the WSP can participate. The sheriff may think it best for all of us to meet. Are you free if we need to set up a meeting tomorrow?"

"I am," said Rick. "Go ahead and set it up. I'm looking forward to seeing the suspects locked up."

Patty sent out a text to all of the team members scheduling a conference call for four P.M. that day. Rick was on the phone, and Patty guessed, based upon Rick's responses, that he was talking with his informant. Patty looked up as the sheriff walked in. "Well, hello Sheriff," Patty said as she stood to shake his hand. "Here to talk about the case?"

"Well, I am here to discuss a case but not the double homicide. You put out a description of Lola Martin's gun last week, and this came in from a Smith River volunteer firefighter." The sheriff laid a gun, carefully wrapped in a plastic bag, down on Patty's desk. It had a numbered tag on it. "I think you'll find that this is consistent with the serial number on her gun. I've signed the chain-of-evidence log, which is there in the folder."

Patty looked at the gun and could see that it was blackened by smoke or soot. "Where'd the firefighter find it?"

"They put out a fire this morning in a small trailer up in the hills off the Smith River south bank. They found evidence of the trailer being used as a meth lab and found this along with three other firearms in the trailer."

Rick was off the phone, heard the exchange, and joined in on the conversation. "So, chances are that the trailer belongs to someone who knows Lola's killer."

"I think that's a safe conclusion," said the sheriff.

Patty looked over at Rick. "Think your informant can give us a name for the owner of the meth lab?"

"I'll ask. It may be the person he's been close to identifying but hasn't given up yet."

The sheriff nodded. "I'm going back to the office and will be on the call at four. But first I have to serve an urgent subpoena for a witness at a grand jury tomorrow."

"Thanks, Sheriff," Patty said.

"The sheriff is a man of few words," Rick observed.

"That's all he has time for," Patty said. "He and his deputies work hard, and they're all underpaid."

"It's three-thirty," Rick said. "I'm going to see if I can get ahold of my informant. Maybe the meth lab fire will spur him to give me a name."

"Let's hope he can give you something," Patty said. "If he gives you a name, run it through Justice and NCIC. The guy will show up in the system if he's been arrested for anything. I've got to get my notes organized for the conference call."

Rick used his cell phone to call the informant, and the call was answered on the second ring. After a few minutes on the phone he interrupted Patty. "My informant's not sure, but he gave me a name and a description," he said, typing into his computer as he input the suspected trailer-owner's name into Justice. "He's in the system for meth use and sales as well as petty theft. I'll contact the agencies here, in Del Norte, Josephine, and Jackson counties. Someone will pick him up."

"That's great," Patty said. "All we need is for him to admit to receiving Lola's gun from Marzi."

Rick nodded. "Guys like that have no problem testifying against someone else as long as they can reduce their own sentence."

At four o'clock Patty initiated the conference call with the Major Crimes Team and shared the new information. "We're going to need help from Federal Way and the WSP," she said. "I'm thinking that we should put together the surveillance plan, and then set up a conference call that includes Detective Sajak and the WSP team, filling them in on how we'd like to carry this out. Any comments?"

"Trooper Jackson here," he said. "The plan sounds good for me. Just let me know where you want me to be and when."

"It's good here, too," said the sheriff. "Patty, you and Rick might want to go with Detective Sajak when he communicates with the possible homeowner victims to vacate their homes for several hours on Sunday. The communication should be done in person and you might want to set up a reception room at the PD or another place where they can talk and enjoy a cup of coffee without becoming upset while they wait."

"Good idea, Sheriff," Patty said. "It's close to five. Let's cut this call now so that I can talk with Sajak and his WSP contact. I'll invite them both to join us on the next call. Can everyone be back on your phone again tomorrow morning at eight thirty?"

With agreement by all on the team, Patty and Rick hung up, and she called Detective Sajak at Federal Way.

"Our thoughts," she said, "would be for me and Rick to join you on Saturday when we can visit each of the prospective victims and ask that they go to a central waiting place immediately after church. I figure the meeting place can be your department's waiting room or some other place that would provide seating and coffee. We can discuss on a call tomorrow morning just when and where each of us will be assigned."

"That will work," he said. "I'll get ahold of WSP about the call tomorrow morning. What time?"

"Eight thirty, if that's not too early," Patty said.

"I'll be available, and I'll see if I can get my state patrol trooper on as well. He also has access to several more troopers he said he could make available to us."

"Great," Patty said. "I'm emailing to you, now, the phone number and access code for the call. Talk with you tomorrow," she said before hanging up.

"Looks like we can call it a day," Patty said.

Before Rick could respond, the radios crackled and both detectives listened as the dispatcher communicated a call from the Del Norte Sheriff's Office for assistance. A deputy stopped a guy for speeding, and as he called it in the guy took off heading north toward Brookings. "The registration gives our burned meth lab trailer as the address," Patty said. A patrol officer and patrol sergeant were already responding, driving south on Highway 101. Patty and Rick got into their car, figuring the guy would be arrested and they'd get the information they need before he was taken back to jail in Crescent City. Rick drove as they listened on their radios to the deputies talking over the sirens. "Elk are on the highway. The suspect's in sight going eighty miles an hour. Oh no! The suspect swerved to avoid the elk and is in the ditch on the side of the road. We need an ambulance, and Fire."

"Oh great!" Rick said as they drove toward the site of the accident. "We need him alive."

Rick pulled the car over, and he and Patty walked up to the accident site to find the suspect slumped over the wheel. Within minutes, Fire arrived and used the Jaws of Life to remove the suspect from his car. Cal-Ore EMTs put the suspect on a stretcher for transport in their ambulance. After placing the stretcher into the back of the ambulance, one EMT looked over at Patty and shook his head as he closed the doors.

Rick and Patty stood in place for a minute before Rick commented. "Would it be insensitive for me to mention I'm glad the elk's okay?" Patty smiled a bit and shrugged her shoulders.

"Well, there goes our chance at keeping Marzi locked up," Rick said.

"Yeah," Patty said. "I'm exhausted. Let's head back to the office and call it a day."

# CHAPTER 17

Their message lights were blinking when Patty and Rick returned to their desks. "I'll pick those up tomorrow," she said. As they prepared to leave, Officer Bradley walked in. "What's up, Brad?"

"We just arrested a guy for shoplifting at a downtown thrift store. He's in bad need of a meth hit and is talking about the trailer in Smith River that just went up in flames. Seems he was living there with the guy who ran his car into a ditch a while ago. Thought you and Rick might want to talk with him. We've got him secured to the table down the hall."

"Thanks, Brad," Patty said. "You just made my day! Rick and I will be right in. Did you admonish him?" She then caught Rick's attention and motioned that it was urgent.

"Brad must have had some good news," Rick said to Patty.

"You're not going to believe this. We may still have a chance to keep Marzi locked up. Seems the guy who ran into the ditch this morning had a partner, and he's now down the hall, picked up for shoplifting."

"Let's go," Rick said pushing away from his desk. "You going to start out?"

"Yeah," Patty said. "He's not yet been admonished so lets talk a minute before going in. I think there's a good chance he'll give up Marzi if we ask the right questions."

"So you're figuring we don't Mirandize him until after he's given us what we need," Rick said.

"Right," Patty said. "And we give up the collar for meth use and distribution."

Rick nodded in agreement. "That works for me. Our need for info about the gun and Marzi far outweighs this guy's admissible statements to meth crimes."

In the interview room the detectives found the suspect handcuffed to the table and finding it impossible to sit still. "Hello," Patty said. "I'm Detective O'Toole and this is Detective Starker. What's your name?"

The suspect moved around in his seat and had an involuntary twitch. "John Welty," he said.

"Thank you, Mr. Welty," Patty said. "What is your home address?"

"I don't have a home address anymore. Like I told the other officer, I was living in a trailer in Smith River that burned down last night."

"We heard that a trailer in Smith River caught fire. What do you think caused the fire?"

The suspect twitched and twisted in his seat. "You must know."

"Maybe, Mr. Welty, but we'd like to hear about it from you," Patty said.

"Oh, man," said Welty. "We were cooking meth, and I really need something or you'll be calling an ambulance soon."

"We just have a few more questions, Mr. Welty. So, you were cooking meth in the trailer. What else did you have in the trailer?"

The suspect grew more and more agitated. "I wasn't cooking the meth. That was Jeb. He'd just trade me some of it for things I'd give him."

Patty glanced up at Rick, who now took the lead. "What kind of things did you trade him, John?"

"Jeb will kill me if I tell you anything else."

"Jeb is dead," Rick said. "And you're probably on your way to being locked up for a long while."

"Dead?" Welty repeated. "Well, I can't go back to prison. Please don't send me back to prison."

"What kinds of things did you trade with, John?" Rick asked again.

"Just stuff I traded with other guys on the street. Jewelry and guns."

"You're doing fine, Mr. Welty," Patty said. "Just a couple more questions and Rick and I will be done here. Where did you get the guns you traded to Jeb?"

"I only traded one gun," he said.

Rick asked, "What kind of gun."

"It was a Glock 19," said the suspect.

"How would you know that it was a Glock 19?" Patty asked.

"Because I know that's what it was. I know other people with Glocks," He said.

"Where'd you get the Glock?" Patty asked.

The suspect twitched and then said, "I didn't steal it if that's what you're thinking. I got it in an honest trade with another guy on the street."

"What other guy?" Patty asked. "We need a name."

The suspect threw his head back and looked at the ceiling. "I only know him as Marzi."

Rick laid a photo of Marzi on the table in front of the suspect.

"Is this Marzi?" Patty asked.

"Yea," replied the suspect.

Patty turned the photo over and handed the suspect a pen. "Please initial here."

The suspect initialed the back of the photo and Patty handed the suspect a yellow tablet. "Now I need you to write down that you got the Glock 19 from Marzi."

\* \* \*

Patty and Rick sat at their desks and briefly discussed the information they now had on the case. "With the identification of Marzi as having given the gun to Welty," Patty said, "I'm going to let the DA know what we have and ask him to keep Marzi locked up until we return from Federal Way and can interview him."

"We're a lot closer to nailing him with Welty's testimony," Rick said.

After talking with the DA Patty let the lieutenant know what they had. His response, as always, was brief. "A few more details and you'll have him," he said. "You still need to prove that Marzi was in the house when Lola was killed."

"Yea, we know. That's going to be tough, so we're hoping this new information springs a confession from Marzi. Rick and I will talk with him when we return."

"Good work, O'Toole, from you and Rick."

"Thanks LT. One more thing. On the subject of the Federal Way surveillance, it'll take Rick and me a day to drive to Federal Way. We'll leave Friday morning after our conference call and plan to drive back on Monday."

The lieutenant nodded toward his assistant in the next room. "I've asked Marcia to help with hotel reservations, so check in with her now so that she can reserve your rooms."

"Okay. We'll take care of it," Patty said before leaving his office and walking back to her desk.

"Now I'm even more exhausted," she said as she gathered her things to go home. "We've got an eight-thirty call tomorrow morning. See you then."

"Okay." Rick said. "I hope Barbara's home when I get there."

Patty looked at Rick. "See you tomorrow."

# CHAPTER 18

Patty arrived at the office early and found Rick busy writing. There was an open bakery bag on the corner of his desk. "Help yourself," he offered.

"I think I will," Patty said. "I overslept a bit and skipped breakfast. I'm going to need a cup of coffee with this," she said, picking up her favorite cup off the desk.

"I wonder if Becky had any idea when she bought it how important that *World's Greatest Mom* cup would be to you?" Rick said.

"Well, I've told her a few times, but she probably won't know how much it really means until she has children of her own. You need a refill?"

"No, I'm good," Rick said as Patty left the room.

At eight thirty Rick and Patty were on the call with the other Major Crimes Team members, in addition to Detective Sajak and two WSP troopers.

"We've got five potential victims," said Sajak, "which allows for two of us at each house if WSP can get us one more trooper."

"Give us the addresses and we'll assign them now," Patty said. "Sheriff and Dan, you want to take the first one?"

Sajak read off the address. "It's off Highway 5 not far from Costco. The second house is in the vicinity of the hospital."

"Give us that address and one more," said the WSP trooper. "I'll recruit two more troopers if Trooper Jackson works with us, and place two of us at each house."

Sajak read off the addresses of the remaining two houses, and they were split up with Patty and Rick at one and Sajak and Kindle at the other. "I've spoken with the manager of our senior center building, which has a room large enough to accommodate all of the homeowners. The manager's been told that we're holding a meeting on public safety. After this call I'll contact the homeowners and let them know we need for them to go to the senior center immediately following the service this Sunday, and why."

Patty spoke up. "It might be better if you wait until Saturday to let them know, Sajak. They're going to need to keep quiet about what we'll be doing, and the less time they have to think about it the better. It would be best to talk with them in person, and Rick and I would like to accompany you on those visits."

"Good point, O'Toole. I'll do that," he replied. "I'll make calls today and schedule appointments for Saturday. If they ask why we want to talk with them, I'll tell them it's about crime in the neighborhood."

"When the suspects are spotted," said the sheriff, "call it in so that the rest of us can provide backup before anyone leaves his car. These guys are armed and dangerous."

"We need to determine positions when arriving at the targeted house," Patty said. "Jackson and the WSP Troopers are the most experienced in this type of entry. What do you suggest?"

"Let's plan it now," said Trooper Jackson. "I'm going to defer to the WSP Troopers to give us our positions. You guys have the most training and experience in this area."

"This is WSP Trooper Landon. My guys will go in first through the front. Sheriff and Ted, position yourselves out front so as to follow us in, if necessary. Patty and Rick and Trooper Jackson, watch the back. Sajak and Detective Jones, remain out front and work with the Sheriff and Ted to stop the suspects if they leave through a side window."

Patty finished up the call, with everyone in agreement on the plan. After the call she and Rick continued their discussion. "We should probably ask Sajak to assign a patrol officer for talking to neighbors if anyone decides to walk out their front door as cars start arriving at the targeted house."

"Reserves would be good for that," Rick said. "I'd suggest two or three if available."

Patty agreed. "I'll pass that on to Sajak."

Patty's desk phone rang. It was the DA, and after a brief conversation she hung up the phone with a smile. "The DA's got a grand jury lined up for Friday. Marzi's not going anywhere. I'm going to let the LT know."

"Nice to get some good news," Rick said.

*   *   *

The lieutenant was in when Patty stopped at his office. "Good to hear the DA's acted so quickly on this. You mentioned a meeting on Tuesday. I'm sure Marzi's attorney, if he's hired one, will recommend a plea deal. How do you feel about that?"

"Well, I guess it will depend," Patty said, "on his intentions when he hit her with the ashtray. He has no prior acts of violence."

"Take time to think it through before making a decision. Starker worked homicides in Boston. Talk with him about his experience before your meeting."

"Okay, LT."

"Anything else, O'Toole?"

Patty shook her head. "No. Rick and I are leaving for Washington early tomorrow."

"You all meeting prior to the church service Sunday morning?" he asked.

"Yes," Patty replied. "We'll meet at the Federal Way PD before taking our respective positions."

The lieutenant stood up. "Good work by you and Rick."

Patty smiled. "Thanks, LT. I'm sure glad we've got a solid suspect for Lola Martin's murder. It seemed so senseless."

The lieutenant agreed. "A lot of them are."

\*    \*    \*

Friday morning Patty arrived to find Rick on his phone. She could tell by hearing his side of the conversation that he was talking with Barbara, and it didn't sound good. She picked up her phone receiver and listened to her voicemail message. Ten minutes later she'd finished noting the last message.

"Ready to go?" she asked when Rick ended his call.

"Yea. I'm looking forward to the drive."

It was a clear, breezy day, making for a beautiful drive between Brookings and Gold Beach.

It was quiet in the car for the first twenty minutes, then Rick spoke up.

"I'm breaking up with Barbara."

Patty was silent a minute, not sure if Rick wanted to say more. "I'm sorry, Rick," she said. "You want to talk about it?"

"Not much to talk about. Barbara's a wonderful woman and will, someday, make some man real happy. The problem is that she's rarely at home when I am. She's asleep when I leave for work in the morning and still at the office when I get home from work. I understand that her job can provide for a twelve-hour-a-day, seven-day-a-week work schedule, but it leaves no time for a private life. I guess I've known for awhile that this couldn't last."

"Have you talked to Barbara about working fewer hours so that the two of you can have a better relationship?"

"I've talked to her several times, and her answer is always the same. I think that I was so grateful to have someone in my life again, when Barbara and I first met, that I figured her long hours wouldn't matter. What I've come to realize is that it does matter." Patty silently looked out the window and let Rick talk. "It hit me the other evening after I explained why Barbara and I couldn't go to the play together. That evening I realized that Barbara and I hadn't done much of anything together since she'd moved in with me."

Patty waited to allow time for Rick to continue and when he didn't, she asked, "How does Barbara feel about breaking up?"

"She's sorry, but she's also devoted to her work. She explained that she didn't realize until recently how much she wanted real estate to be her career. She also said that she realizes how little time she's spending with me and that she understands I have a need for someone whose work can accommodate my hours. She said she'd begin looking for an apartment and can move in with a girlfriend of hers, another real estate agent, until she finds a place of her own."

"I know this is hard for you, Rick. Barbara was the first woman you really dated since Claire died. I'm sure there are a lot of other women out there who would love to make a home with you."

Rick looked over at Patty. "Thanks," he said.

"We've got a lot going on right now, Rick. You okay?"

Rick's expression changed from the sad, concerned look to one of control. "Yea. I'm fine. After losing Claire and Skylar, this is hardly a two on the one-to-ten trauma scale. I'm ready to take down the suspects we'll meet up with on Sunday."

Patty smiled. "Someday, Rick, a lucky woman will find that you're a great catch, and she'll want to spend evenings with you and do things like attend a Saturday play."

Rick couldn't help himself and grinned wide. "You mean like the play date, I mean the date at the play we're going on?" Patty rolled her eyes as she ignored the comment.

Thirty minutes out of Brookings, Rick said, "It's less than four hours to Yachats. How about we stop there for lunch?"

Patty laughed. We're barely out of Brookings and you're already thinking about lunch? And Yachats is pronounced 'YAH hots.' It's a Chinook Indian word meaning 'dark waters at the foot of the mountain.'"

"Thanks. I just like to know when we're going to eat, and Yachats has a great seafood restaurant. It's called the Luna Sea Fish House."

"Lunacy Fish House?" Patty asked. "I wonder why?"

Rick smiled. "It's owned by the Lunas, and the name is spelled Luna Sea."

"That's a great play on words," Patty said. "Driving to Federal Way up the coast to Yachats is going to add two hours to our trip, getting to our hotel at, maybe, seven, including time for lunch. That going to work for you?"

"No problem," Rick said. "It's a great drive."

"Well, I'm up for it," said Patty, "and as long as we're stopping in Yachats, I want to stop in at Mari's Book Store. It's been a few years since I was there, but I remember it being a very pleasant experience."

"Time shouldn't be a problem," Rick said. "I figure we'll pull into Federal Way just in time for dinner. Of course we may be a little later if we stop for ice cream in Tillamook."

"Let's see if we have room for ice cream after our Luna Sea experience," Patty laughed. "If we don't stop in Tillamook on our way, we can always have an ice cream on the way home."

"We'll see," said Rick. "So it's Yachats," he said pronouncing it correctly. "There sure is a lot of Indian influence in Oregon city names."

"That's because the Indians lived along the Oregon coast before the Caucasians," Patty said. "According to the stories I've read, it wasn't until the mid-1800s that the Native Indian dominance in this area came to an end. There's a great book out called *Chetco,* by Mike Adams. If you're interested in learning more about the history of Curry County I have a copy that I can loan you."

"Thanks. I'm interested. It'll be good reading once this weekend is over."

Driving through an area of thick forest, Rick could see smoke wafting through the trees. "There must be a house back there," he said, "with a fireplace. It's kind of spooky the way that smoke crawls amongst the trees and across the highway. Kind of goes hand-in-hand with our homicides."

"There's murder on the wind," Patty said as she stared out the window.

# CHAPTER 19

Arriving in Federal Way the detectives located their hotel. "We're set to meet with Sajak at the police station at nine thirty tomorrow," Patty said. "He has appointments set up at all five houses. Sunday everyone will meet at eight, which should give us plenty of time to review our plan, and for everyone to get into place before the targeted homeowners leave for church."

"It's great that everyone is so well organized," Rick said. "You want to have dinner here after we've checked into our rooms?"

"I'm still pretty full from lunch," Patty said, "but I could use something warm like a cup of soup. I'll meet you in the restaurant at seven. That'll give me time to call Becky and check my email."

"Okay," Rick said. "See you then."

At seven the detectives sat down for dinner in the hotel restaurant. "Do you think there's a chance the suspects won't show Sunday?" Rick asked.

"Well, there's always a chance, but I don't know why they wouldn't continue as they've done in the past. The fact that they went to the trouble of setting up someone here to obtain addresses of the church parishioners suggests that they're intent upon working their scam for all it's worth."

"Yea, I agree," said Rick. "It's great that the WSP have their own Investigation Assistance Division. We'd have had a difficult time locating enough law enforcement to cover all five homes if they hadn't come through for us."

"I agree," Patty said. "I wonder if Trooper Jackson will take the information back to the OSP after working with Washington's troopers? Maybe set up an Investigative Services Bureau in Oregon."

Rick nodded. "Oregon seems to be lacking in several areas, including their processing of fingerprints."

Finished with their dinner, Patty flagged the waitress that they were done.

As they left the restaurant Patty said, "Breakfast here starts at six. I'll meet you in the front lobby at seven."

*       *       *

At eight A.M. Sunday morning, the ten law-enforcement members involved in the surveillance effort met at the Federal Way Police Station. They spent the first fifteen minutes introducing themselves while they drank coffee and enjoyed an array of pastries.

Patty tapped her spoon against a glass to get everyone's attention. "Thank you all for being here and participating in this surveillance," she said. "Yesterday, Detectives Sajak and Starker and I spoke with the homeowners of our five targeted homes, and they'll all go to the senior center following their church service." Patty then addressed Sajak. "Anything you'd like to add?"

"Sure. The residents understood that they were not to talk with anyone about the reason we need them to stay clear of their homes for a couple of hours. I've got two reserve officers who will stay with them and answer questions as they arise."

"Thanks, Detective," Patty said. "The suspects we're after have, as you know, burglarized a number of homes in Oregon and Washington and have killed four people that we know of. You've all got your assigned locations. We can expect the suspects to arrive at their chosen home within ten minutes one side or the other of ten o'clock, which is when the church service starts. They'll be armed and extremely dangerous. WSP has distributed portable radios to each of you, and they're set to a common tactical channel. Remember to use plain language for all transmissions when communicating. No radio codes since we're from different states. We'll identify each other by using only our last names. If the suspects show up at the home you're watching, contact me immediately and do not leave your vehicle until backup has arrived. I'll want to know the complete street address, how many suspects entered the house, brief descriptions of the suspects, and whether any of them have remained outside of the house. I'll then use the radio, give the phrase, 'Mission is a go,' and transfer the information on the suspects. We all want this to be completed without injury or loss of life. If a fellow officer is hurt, the quickest way to get help may be for you to drive him or her to the hospital rather than wait for an ambulance. Therefore Detective Sajak has given you each a map of the nearest medical facility to each targeted house. Any questions?"

Sheriff's Detective Dan Jones stood up. "That's all good information, O'Toole. I have one additional thought we might want to consider. It is possible that more than one of these homes will be burglarized at the same time. Therefore we may need to have one of every two assigned to a targeted house remain at that house, rather than going immediately to the address at which the first suspects show up."

"That's a good point, Jones," Patty said. "Let's have each team determine now who will stay at the assigned house. This will reduce our numbers to a half dozen responding to the targeted house, which should be sufficient." Patty paused during the brief discussion and then proceeded. "Any other comments or questions?"

One of the reserve officers raised his hand. "You want us to use lights and sirens?" he asked.

"Use your lights and sirens only if necessary. We don't want these guys to get spooked and flee the scene before enough of us can get there."

Trooper Jackson then called out, "You want us to meet back here when we're finished at the target?"

"Yes," Patty said.

# CHAPTER 20

At nine thirty Rick and Patty sat in their unmarked car, a few cars down from the house to which they were assigned. Twenty-five minutes later Patty's portable radio came alive. "This is the sheriff, Patty. There are three of them and all have exited a black van and have entered the house. All three are Caucasian and wearing blue jeans and black sweatshirts with some insignia on the front. No hats."

The sheriff then gave Patty the address of the house, and she responded. "We're on our way." Rick started up the car and pulled out from the curb as Patty got on the radio. "Mission is a go," she said before providing a house address and the description of the suspects.

Because of the close proximity of the five homes everyone arrived within two minutes at the targeted house and fell into their assigned positions. Rick and Patty followed the WSP troopers into the house and heard gunfire almost immediately. Two of the suspects were in the master bedroom, where one was pouring the contents of a jewelry box into a cloth bag and the other had been searching a bedside table. The suspect searching the table had pulled his gun on the first WSP Trooper to enter the room, was shot twice, and now lay on the floor. The other suspect dropped the bag of jewelry and put up his hands, surrendering. The third suspect climbed through the window of a second bedroom where he was apprehended and cuffed by Detective Jones. The rest of the house was searched to make sure another suspect hadn't entered from the back. Finding it all secure, Patty radioed for an ambulance. "We've got a victim with two gunshot wounds, and I don't have a pulse," she said as she leaned down and placed two of her fingers against the man's carotid artery. She then assigned CPR to the officer standing next to her and walked to the front of the house where Detective Sajak was talking with his reserves.

"Can your reserves stay," Patty asked, "to keep everyone out of the house until the ambulance and your guys arrive to process the scene?"

"Sure," he said. "I'll talk with them now and see you back at my office. I've also sent an officer over to the church to pick up the volunteer parking attendant. The officers at the senior center are being briefed on what's happened. They'll let everyone, except for the couple who own this house, go home. The owners of this house will be taken to the station, where they'll be briefed and given information about the nearest business that does cleanup. We'll put them up in a hotel for a few days while we finish up at the crime scene and the place is cleaned."

"Great," Patty said. "Rick and I will want to interview the suspects. Can you let them sit in a cell until after lunch?"

"I was planning on it," Sajak said. "I'm hungry myself, and chances are pretty good they'll just lawyer up."

"Most likely," Patty said. "We'll head back to your office now for a quick follow-up briefing and then take off to eat. You have lunch plans?"

"Yea, I'm going to eat with the WSP guys. Maybe learn more about their special crime unit."

"Okay," Patty said before walking over to Rick, who was standing next to their car talking with one of the reserves.

"That went well," Rick said to Patty as they got into the car.

"Like a well-made plan," she replied. "Federal Way will probably want to try the two surviving suspects in their courts here before sending them back to us, which shouldn't be a problem. After lunch we'll interview them, but I don't expect to get far before they invoke their rights."

"Yeah," said Rick, "but with the similarities in the rope, knots, and gun, we should have enough to put them away for a long time."

At the Federal Way offices, Patty thanked everyone for their assistance and cooperation. "We've removed some pretty dangerous thugs from the streets today. I want to thank you all, and give a special thanks to Detective Sajak, who entered the details of the Federal Way murders into the ViCAP system. We may not have caught these guys before they killed again if it hadn't been for ViCAP matching the rope, knots, and gun."

"Thanks for telling us about that," said Trooper Johnson. "We'd kind of gotten away from using it because of the cumbersome need to enter so much information. It's clear, however, that it paid off here, so I'll mention it in my report and suggest we try it again."

Patty and Rick invited the sheriff, Detective Jones, and Deputy Kindle to go to lunch with them. "Sajak gave Rick the names of a couple good restaurants," she said.

Rick pulled the list out of his pocket. "Do you want Mexican or diner food?"

They all opted for Mexican. "We'll take our own car," said the sheriff. "We need to head south after eating."

"Sure," said Patty. During lunch, Patty and Rick talked to the others about the Lola Martin case. "We've got a witness," Patty said, "who will testify to having received from Marzi the same type of gun that was purchased by the victim. And we have a witness who will testify that Marzi came into a sudden windfall of cash about the time Lola Martin was killed. What we don't have, yet, is a way to prove that Marzi was in that house and killed Lola Martin."

"Have you had a criminalist or ballistics expert confirm that it's the same gun?" asked the sheriff.

"Nothing yet," Rick said. "Do you know how backed up Oregon is?"

"Yeah," said the sheriff, "I've heard that a lot."

Patty's cell phone rang, and she read the caller's name. "It's my daughter," she said. "Excuse me a minute. Hi Bec," Patty said. "Can I call you back later this afternoon?"

"Not a problem, Mom. Just want you to know I got one of the scholarships I applied for. I'll tell you about it later."

"Becky, that's wonderful! I'll look forward to hearing all about it."

"Talk with you later, Mom," Becky said before hanging up.

Patty looked over at Rick, who was waiting for the wonderful news. "Becky learned that she's received one of three scholarships for which she applied."

"That is great news," said Rick.

"She still want to be a vet?" asked the sheriff.

Patty grinned. "She sure does, and this will help a lot toward tuition for the next couple of years."

"Good for her," said Jones. "Maybe Becky could talk to my daughter, Megan. She's a high school junior and still has no clue as to what she wants to do after college."

"I'm sure Becky would love to discuss college plans with Megan," Patty said. "Talk with her, and if she's serious just let me know. I'll give you Becky's cell phone number for Megan."

"Thanks," said Jones. "I'll do that."

After lunch Patty and Rick drove back to the Federal Way PD, where they met with the suspects individually. "You know what the prison sentence is for a felony murder charge?" Patty asked each of them. As expected, both suspects asked for a lawyer rather than answer any questions.

Detective Sajak walked with Patty and Rick out to their car. "I'll keep you abreast of the trial dates here. We may need one or both of you to testify to the burglaries and murders in Brookings."

"No problem," Patty said. "We may need the same from you when we try them in Curry County."

"Thanks for the tips on the restaurants," Rick told Sajak. "The Mexican food was great!"

On their drive back to Brookings, Patty and Rick discussed the successful capture of the suspects who'd killed four people and burglarized many others in two states.

"That's the largest group of law enforcement staged at one surveillance setting that I've ever been part of," Patty said. "It was great working on the same project with so many good people."

Rick nodded as he drove. "I worked with a large group several times, but they were all from Boston PD. This was unique for me to have several agencies involved. It may be the start of agencies in Oregon and Washington working together on more crimes where the suspects are travelling in both states."

"And now we're back to dealing with the Lola Martin murder," Patty said. "Our interview tomorrow is with Marzi at nine. What are your thoughts on how he's going to respond?"

"Well," Rick said, "it's hard to say. Like you were explaining at lunch, we think we can link him to both Lola Martin's gun and a large amount of money immediately following her death. Is that enough for him to confess? I don't know."

"The evidence would be a whole lot stronger," Patty said, "if our witnesses weren't all drug addicts. The defense attorney is going to latch on to that and attempt to prove that the witnesses could be lying in order to collect the small reward."

"So how do we get Marzi to talk?" Rick asked.

"I'll be the good cop to your bad," Patty said.

Rick smiled. "I wouldn't want it any other way. Got any idea as to how you'll approach him?"

"Yeah, I think I do," Patty said. "If need be, I'm going to remind him of his criminal record thus far, and educate him on the difference between murder one and manslaughter."

"Okay," Rick said. "I've got to change the subject now because we're coming into Tillamook and there's a Tillamook Mudslide ice cream cone with my name on it at the creamery. You up for stopping?"

"Sure. I love their ice cream, and I'd like to take home some cheese to share with Becky, Mom, and Bill. Do you know the history of the Tillamook Creamery?"

"A little of it," Rick said. "I know it's made up of a cooperative of about a hundred dairy farmers."

"It's been farmer owned since 1909," Patty said. "There are five rivers flowing into Tillamook Bay, and that abundance of water, along with the constant rainfall, made the land perfect for dairy farming. Prior to roads and the highway being built, the cheese was transferred by boat up the ocean and across the Columbia River to Portland."

"They transfer milk, too?" Rick asked.

"No. My understanding is that milk would not have kept long enough for the boat to get to Portland. That's no longer a problem, of course."

"Looks like they're doing some remodeling," Rick said as they pulled into the parking lot. "They probably had to make it bigger to accommodate all the tourists."

The detectives found a table where they sat down to eat their ice cream.

Patty's cell phone rang. "It's mom," she said, putting her spoon down. "Hi Mom. What's up?"

"Well, I've been eager to learn what's going on with you and Rick. All you said before leaving was that you had a case in Washington. After all these years, I know that you and Rick wouldn't be sent to Washington for several days unless it was for something really big. There was a short story on the noon news about a shootout in a home in Federal Way. I'm guessing you and Rick were part of that. Am I right?"

Patty looked up at Rick as she continued to speak to her mother. "We were up here for that case, Mom, but we're both fine and on our way back to Brookings. I'll tell you about it when I get home."

"On the news they said that one of the suspects was shot and killed. Was it you or Rick that got the guy?"

"Neither of us, Mom. I can't talk anymore now because my ice cream is melting. I'll talk with you tonight."

"Ice cream? Where are you?"

"In Tillamook, Mom, and we've got to leave. Rick's already done with his cone. See you tonight."

"Okay, dear. Tell Rick I'm glad you got the bad guys. Careful driving back."

Patty walked to the counter to get a plastic cup and turned her cone upside down into it. She asked for a plastic spoon and walked back to the table. "I'm ready," she said. "I'll finish this in the car."

"From what I could tell, your mom saw something on the news about Federal Way," Rick said.

"Yeah. No telling how much of what she saw was accurate. I'll talk with her tonight."

"Going to tell her about tomorrow's interview?" Rick asked, smiling.

"Not a chance," Patty said.

# CHAPTER 21

At nine the next day, Patty and Rick walked into the interview room where Marzi and his attorney sat waiting. The detectives introduced themselves and sat with their backs to the two-way mirror.

"We're here to discuss your association with Lola Martin," Patty said. "How well did you know her?"

"She was my friend's sister," Marzi said.

"What's the name of your friend?"

"Spencer Martin," Marzi said.

"How did you know that Lola Martin was Spencer's sister?"

"What do you mean how did I know?" Marzi asked.

Patty asked the question a little differently. "Had you met her while visiting your friend at his home? Or, had you been to Lola's house?"

The suspect shifted in his seat. "I met her once at Spencer's house."

"What did you think of her when you met her?" Patty asked.

"I don't know," Marzi responded. "I really didn't think about it. She was just his sister."

"Are you sure that's all she meant to you?" Patty asked. "I heard you had a bit of a crush on her."

Marzi laughed. "A crush? No, I wouldn't call it a crush. She was pretty, okay?"

Patty smiled. "Did you want to take care of her? Want her to move in with you?"

Marzi laughed again. "I wasn't her type. And she had a nice house and everything. Much better than what I had. She'd of never moved in with me."

"You mean that she had the kind of house with more than one bedroom, and a nice living area?"

"Yeah, I guess so," Marzi said.

Patty nodded. "She probably had made it pretty, too, with things like lamps and ashtrays."

Marzi hesitated looking into Patty's eyes. He then smiled. "I told you I'd never been in her house. I don't know what kinds of things she had."

Patty and Rick locked eyes, and Rick then spoke to Marzi. "We happen to know that you traded a gun to John Welty for drugs. Where'd you get the gun?"

"I don't know what you're talking about," Marzi said.

"Welty will take the witness stand and testify that he received a Glock 19 from you in exchange for drugs."

Marzi's attorney looked surprised and leaned over to speak with his client. "You didn't tell me about any gun," he said.

Marzi sat back in his chair. "If that's all they have on me it won't stick. I trade stuff all the time and don't remember everything I traded."

Rick leaned back in his chair. "You were spending money a few weeks ago like it was water. Where'd you get it?"

Now it was Marzi's turn to look surprised as he sat up. "I don't know what you mean."

"Yeah, I think you do," Rick said. "We've got at least two people who will testify to your having a wad of hundred dollar bills just shortly after Lola Martin was killed."

"Yeah. That was money I'd saved up."

Now Rick leaned forward and stared into Marzi's eyes. "Do you know the difference between being charged with murder or involuntary manslaughter?"

"I didn't murder Lola Martin," Marzi said.

"You had a gun like hers, and suddenly, after her death, came into a lot of money," Rick said. "We think you got that from Lola's house after you murdered her. If you didn't murder Lola, how'd you get her gun and the money?"

Marzi was now having a hard time sitting still. His attorney leaned over and whispered something to him that made Marzi shake his head violently. "No," he yelled. "I got that gun from her brother after he murdered Lola. He gave me the money to keep quiet."

Rick and Patty glanced at each other. Then Rick continued. "Lola's brother loved his sister. He wouldn't have murdered her. You learned she had her savings in her house and you went there to get that money, but you didn't expect she'd be home. That's what happened. Isn't it?"

"He's given you the murderer, Detectives," said Marzi's attorney. "You've got nothing to place my client in Lola Martin's home at the time of the murder. My client's not saying anything else."

Rick and Patty got up and walked out of the interview room and back to their offices. "I'll go talk to the LT," Patty said.

"I'm going to see if there's doughnuts in the break room," said Rick.

In the lieutenant's office Patty explained how the interview went with Marzi and then walked back to her office, where she found Rick had refilled their coffee cups and put a couple cookies and a napkin on her desk.

"No doughnuts," he said, "but I thought you could use these."

"Thanks," she said, picking up one of the cookies. "Do you think there's any truth to his accusation?"

Rick shook his head. "No. But without evidence that Marzi was in that house, it will be hard to get a conviction."

"Yeah," Patty said before picking up her coffee cup. "Have you heard anything else from your informant that might suggest it wasn't Marzi?"

"Only that he's got nothing more for us," Rick said.

Patty folded her hands on top of her desk. "Okay. We need to talk again with Spencer Martin. You want to call and find out if he's going to be down here? If not, let's go up there tomorrow, if he's home. I need to listen to my phone messages and check emails from the past three days."

Rick called and spoke with Spencer Martin and waited until Patty hung up her phone receiver. "We've got a two o'clock appointment to talk with Mr. Martin tomorrow at his place. Needless to say he's not too keen on being interviewed again."

"What else does he have to do?" Patty asked. "That was rhetorical. It takes about three hours to get to Reedsport, so we need to leave by eleven."

"Let's leave at ten," said Rick, "That will give us time to eat lunch at Redfish, in Port Orford."

"Great idea," Patty said. "Don't you love their Hawthorne Gallery?"

"Gallery?" Rick asked.

Patty sat back in her chair. "You mean you've eaten at Redfish but never been in their art gallery?"

"You act like I've committed some kind of mortal sin!" Rick said. "Art galleries have just never interested me much."

"Okay. I'm sorry. It's just hard for me to imagine that you'd eat lunch at Redfish and not take time to tour the gallery."

"Well," Rick said, "how many times have you toured the Hawthorne Gallery and not, immediately before or after, eaten at Redfish?"

"A few, I guess."

Rick knew he had her. "Well, it's hard for me to imagine that you'd tour the gallery and not eat at the adjoining restaurant."

Patty smiled. "Point made," she said.

Rick smiled. "We've got a little time left today so I'm going to work on my report about our Federal Way case."

"I need to do the same," Patty said, "but not today. Right now I'm going to make a courtesy call to the chief in Reedsport so that he knows the nature of our visit tomorrow with Spencer Martin."

# CHAPTER 22

The next morning Patty and Rick took off for Reedsport again. "Reedsport's chief will provide backup for us while we're at Mr. Martin's," Patty said. "They have a smaller agency than we do, so he's only got one patrol officer on the day shift. He'll ask his officer to cover incoming calls while he's available to us."

As they traveled up Highway 101, smoke came through the trees, wafting its way across the highway. "There's that smoke riding on the wind, again," Rick said. "Must be a house just beyond these trees. What was that you said the last time we saw it?"

Patty looked over at Rick. "I said there's murder on the wind."

Rick nodded. "I like that."

*   *   *

Spencer Martin opened the front door as the detectives walked up the steps to his porch. "I don't mind talking with you, again, Detectives," he said, "but maybe you can tell me why you want to talk again with me? I heard you've got Marzi in jail. Did he confess to murdering my sister?"

Patty and Rick walked through the front door into the living room and sat in the same place they'd sat the first time they spoke with Spencer Martin. "Well," Patty said, "I don't know what you heard, but we have no confession. As a matter of fact, Marzi seems to know who killed your sister and gave us a name."

"He told you someone else did it?" Martin blurted out. "Who?"

Patty looked at Rick who then responded. "You, Mr. Martin. Marzi said it was you who killed Lola, stole her money and gun."

"Me?" the otherwise quiet man shouted as he jumped up from his chair. "That SOB! He knows I'd never hurt Lola. He's lying to save his own skin."

"That may be," Rick said. "But we need you to tell us again where you were the evening your sister was killed. Do you remember that day?"

"I'll never forget that day, Detective," Martin said. "I was here most of the day. I might have driven over to the Dairy Queen for something to eat. But I was here at home the rest of the time."

Rick looked at his notes. "You went to the Dairy Queen? That's not what you told us when we were here before. You said then that you hadn't left the house."

Spencer Martin stood up and began to pace the floor. "I can't remember everything I told you then. I was pretty upset and had smoked some weed that day. It only just now occurred to me that I may have gone to Dairy Queen."

"Smoking weed is habit forming, isn't it?" Patty asked. "It takes money to continue that habit. Where do you get the money, Spencer?"

"I work now and then on the fishing boats and put my money away," he said.

"From what I hear, working on the fishing boats doesn't bring in enough money to sustain a weed habit," Rick said.

Spencer sat down again across from the detectives. "I do odd jobs for people now and then if I need more cash. I get by."

Rick stared with steel-blue eyes at Spencer. "You must have thought about all that cash under your sister's mattress, Spencer. Did it ever make you mad that she was able to hold down a good-paying job and accumulate so much cash? Did you think that some of it ought to be yours?"

"That money was Lola's and, no, I never thought that any of it should be mine. She deserved everything she had."

Patty and Rick silently stared at Spencer Martin, who stared at the floor. After a minute of silence Spencer started talking. "I was pretty sure Marzi killed Lola. But if he didn't, what about that guy she worked with?"

"What guy?" Patty asked.

"Some guy she worked with. Lola told me once she had a friend at work who did odd jobs a couple times at her house for her. His name was Glen, Tim, or Ben. Ben, that was it. Have you spoken to him?"

Patty and Rick looked at each other. "We'll make note of his name," Patty said. "Is there anything Lola said about Ben that makes you think he could have killed her?"

"Well, not exactly. I guess it just seemed kind of odd that he would help her out that way, unless he wanted to be more than a friend."

"Are you sure that he was ever at Lola's house?" Rick asked.

"Yeah, I'm sure. Lola mentioned it to me when she visited last December. She said he was always offering to help her out, so she let him come over a couple times to fix things in the house. I suppose she could have told him about her money."

"All right. That's all we have for now," Rick said as he and Patty stood up. "We'll be in touch if we need to talk with you again."

In their car on the drive home, Patty and Rick discussed the new information. Rick drove while Patty looked at her notes from the interview with Ben Brown.

"Ben said he'd never been in Lola's house," Patty said. "I should have a cell signal until we're out of Reedsport. I'll set up an appointment for us to talk with him tomorrow morning. I'm surprised that he'd lie if he had nothing to do with the murder."

Rick let out a slight laugh. "I guess I've been doing this for too long, Patty. Nothing people say surprises me anymore."

Patty called Fred Meyer and a woman at the service desk picked up. "May I help you?"

"Yes, thank you. This is Brookings Detective O'Toole calling for Ben Brown."

"I'm afraid Mr. Brown isn't available," she said.

"Then I'd like to speak with his supervisor Karen Gains."

"I'll ring Ms. Gains for you," said the helpful woman.

Ms. Gains picked up on the second ring. "This is Ms. Gains. May I help you?"

"Ms. Gains, this is Detective O'Toole. Before I go on, let me tell you that I'm on my way south from Reedsport and on a cell phone. If the call is dropped I'll call back when I can."

"I understand, Detective," she said. "Happens to me all the time when I'm travelling along the coast. What can I do for you?"

I'm calling because Detective Starker and I need to schedule an appointment tomorrow morning with Ben Brown. Can you arrange that?"

"Oh, Detective, I'm sorry, but Mr. Brown no longer works here."

"No longer works there?" Patty asked, looking over at Rick, who glanced her way. "Why did he leave?"

"Well, he told me that he had a sick relative in California who he had to help out. It was all very sudden, and he didn't even give us the requested two-weeks' notice."

"Ms. Gains, can you tell me the date of Ben Brown's last day of work?" Patty asked.

"I'll look up the date, but I can tell you it was two days after you interviewed Ben and me."

"Did he give you a forwarding address for his last paycheck?" Patty asked.

"He did. I can look that up too." Before Patty could respond the call was dropped. "I'll call her again when we're back in the office. By then she'll have the date of his last work day and his forwarding address," Patty said.

"Looks like we'll be making a quick trip to California," Rick said. "I hope it's the northern end. There's just too much traffic in the southern part of the state."

# CHAPTER 23

After returning to their office, Patty called Karen Gains for the date of Ben's last workday and his forwarding address. "We won't have to travel far," she said to Rick. "Ben's forwarding address is in Willits. Gains gave me his cell phone number, too."

"Willits," Rick said. "I've never been there but I believe it's on 101. Do you know it?"

"I do," Patty said. "It's about a five-hour drive from here, and for your information, is equipped with both a Burger King and a McDonalds."

"My kind of town," Rick said. "You going to call him and set something up for tomorrow?"

"Yeah, if we go and come back tomorrow it'll be about a twelve-hour day. I'm up for it and can share the driving if that works for you. We can leave here at eight."

"Works for me. I'll pick up a few doughnuts on the way in. We can take them with us in the car."

"Okay," Patty said. "But no powdered sugar," she said with a smile. "I'll try getting Ben Brown on the phone now."

"Hello?" said the voice on the other end of the line.

"Hello Mr. Brown. This is Detective O'Toole. Do you remember me and my partner Detective Starker?"

"Of course I do," he said. "Why are you calling?"

"We've received some new information about the death of Lola Martin, and we need to talk again with you."

"Well, I've moved and don't live in Brookings," he said.

"We know that, Mr. Brown. We understand that you're now living in Willits, California. Is that right?"

"Well, yes it is. I'm living with my uncle," he said.

"Detective Starker and I can meet you in Willits tomorrow at two. Just let us know where you want to meet."

"I'd rather you not come to my uncle's house, Detective. He's not well. What new information do you have that makes it necessary for you to talk again with me?"

"I can't discuss the information over the phone with you, Mr. Brown. Why don't we meet at the Burger King? It should be pretty quiet at that time of day."

Patty listened and hearing no response, spoke again. "We need to meet with you Mr. Brown. Detective Starker and I will meet you tomorrow at the Burger King at two o'clock. Will you be there?"

"Yeah, I'll be there," said Brown.

"Thank you," Patty said. "Goodbye."

Patty hung up the phone and looked at the time. "I need to call Willits' chief before I leave," she said. "Let him know we're coming tomorrow and why. This has been one heck of a day."

"And we still don't have Lola Martin's killer," Rick added.

"Yeah, but we will," Patty said as she put her files away.

*   *   *

Patty and Rick met in the office and then began their drive to Willits. "Have you been to Trees of Mystery," Patty asked Rick as they passed the decades-old tourist attraction.

"No, I've thought about it several times," Rick said. "But I don't have much reason to drive south on 101. I'm realizing, again, as we travel through these redwoods, how beautiful a drive it is."

"There's a lot of history along this coast," Patty said. "We'll drive through McKinleyville, where materials were purchased to help build the St. George Reef Lighthouse. As with Oregon, most of these small towns on 101 have an interesting past."

"Yeah?" said Rick. "Well, don't hesitate to educate me along the way."

"You got it," Patty said.

After a comfortable five-hour drive, they arrived in Willits, where Patty directed Rick to the Burger King. "We've got an hour to eat before our interview. Willits' chief sent me an email, and like Reedsport, he'll provide backup while his patrol officer answers local calls."

"Good," Rick said. "That gives me time to eat a proper lunch."

"A proper lunch?" Patty asked. "What makes a lunch proper?"

"More than just a burger," Rick said with a smile. "I'm going to have fries and a shake too."

Patty just laughed. "Why does that not surprise me?" she said.

They ordered and sat down at a corner table where Patty and Rick could sit with a clear view of the doors. "So," Rick said, "how do you want to do this?"

Patty smiled. "Why don't you take the lead," she said.

"Wow!" Rick said. "You're going to let me be good cop?"

"I didn't say that," Patty said, smiling. "I just suggested that you take the lead with questioning. Let's see where it goes."

When lunch was delivered, Rick started in on his burger while Patty stuck a fork in her salad. After eating, they discussed the questions they'd ask the suspect.

Ben Brown arrived at two and walked back to the table where the detectives were seated. The Willits police chief sat in his marked car in the parking lot.

"Hello Ben," Rick said. "We appreciate your meeting with us again."

"You must think I had something to do with Lola's death," Ben said, "for you to drive down here from Brookings. What is it you want to know?"

"We need to ask you, again, Ben. Where you were the day Lola was killed?"

"I was at home. Alone. And no, I can't prove that I was."

Rick's facial expression did not change. "You sure you didn't leave for an hour or so, Ben?"

"I'm sure," the young man said, looking down at the table.

"How long did it take you to drive from your house to Lola's?" Rick asked.

Ben lifted his head and looked first at Rick and then to Patty. "I told you before that I never went to Lola's house, so how would I know?"

"We think your memory may not be serving you well, Ben," said Rick. "We think you'd gone to Lola's house more than once to help her with something that needed to be fixed. We have a witness who will testify to that, Ben."

Tears welled up in the young man's eyes. "Okay," he said. "I was there a couple of times, but only because Lola asked me over."

"What did you do while you were there, Ben?" Rick asked. "Did you and Lola have something going on?"

"It was nothing like that," Ben said. "Lola didn't want me in that way. She just liked me as a friend and knew I liked to help her with fixing things around the house."

"Did it make you mad that Lola didn't want you to be more than a friend? Maybe make you want to fix it so that no one else could have Lola?" Rick asked.

"I know where you're going with this," Ben said. "I didn't kill Lola. She was my friend. I wish you'd just leave me alone now and go find her killer."

The detectives locked eyes, and Patty leaned forward while Rick sat back.

"Did Lola show you where she kept her money?" Patty asked.

"What money?" Ben asked.

"Come on, Ben. You were Lola's friend. I'm sure she must have confided in you about things like her savings. She must have told you about how she was saving for her future."

"We didn't have conversations about money other than our pay and benefits at work. I guess she told me that she saved most of her money, so I figured she had a savings account. I guess that was one of the ways that we were alike. I like to save my money too."

"It would help," Patty said, "if you showed us your last few savings account statements."

"Why?" Ben asked. "It's none of your business."

"It would help us to believe you," said Rick. "We'd see that there wasn't a big deposit after Lola died. If you want, we could get a warrant. But that just means we'll need to talk with you again."

Ben sat up straight and raised his voice. "You think I'd kill Lola for her money?"

"We're investigating Lola's murder," Patty said. "And we need to cover all the bases."

Ben pulled out his cell phone, typed on it a few times, and turned the phone around so that Patty and Rick could see the screen. "I'll show you right now," he said. "This is my bank statement for the month Lola was killed." After the detectives had a chance to review it, Ben showed them past statements up to the most recent.

"Okay," Patty said. "Thanks for showing those to us, Ben."

"Did Lola ever mention a guy named Marzi?" Rick asked.

Ben's immediate response was negative, but then he paused. "You know, I think maybe that's what she called the creepy guy who she said showed up at her house a couple of times. I think he knows Lola's brother."

Patty and Rick glanced at each other and then stood up. "Thanks for your time," Rick said. "You've been very helpful. We'll let you know if we need to talk again with you."

Before the detectives walked away, Patty turned again to Ben. "I hope that your uncle's health improves."

Patty walked over to the chief before meeting Rick back at their car. "Thanks, Chief," she said. "Were you able to check on the address we gave you?"

"Yeah. The house belongs to a Roger Brown. My officer's lived here all his life and says that Roger's an okay guy, far as he knows. Roger's also got terminal cancer. You learn anything from your interview?"

"Yeah," Patty said. "We don't see him for it. I think we've got the right guy locked up in Gold Beach." Patty held up her right hand, bringing her thumb and first fingers almost together. We're this close to putting him away for a long time."

"Good luck," said the chief.

"Thanks," Patty said before walking over to the unmarked car to join Rick, who was already seated in the driver's side.

The detectives drove out of the Burger King parking lot and turned north onto the highway.

"This used to be a pretty crowded town to drive through," Patty said. "The shops appeared to do a lot of business. With the new highway put in last year, Willits has become a ghost of what it was."

"I guess that's progress," Rick said. "What's your thought on Ben Brown?"

"What do we know about him?" Patty asked.

"Well," Rick said. "He worked with the deceased, initially lied to us about going to Lola's house, quit his job, and moved immediately after Lola died."

Patty interrupted, "Because he had to care for his sick uncle in Willits."

"And now," Rick continued, "admits to being in her home but denies being any more than a friend."

"And?" Patty asked.

"And I believe him," Rick said. "You?"

"I believe him too," Patty said. "Which leaves us with Marzi or Spencer Martin."

About an hour into their drive north, Patty's cell phone chimed. Looks like a call came in while we were in a no cell-service area. It's from OSP.

Garberville's just up ahead. How about pulling over so that I can listen to the message before we're out of cell range again?"

Rick saw the Garberville sign and pulled off the highway, driving up the road to where he could park and check his own phone for messages while Patty listened to hers.

Two minutes later Patty put her phone down and looked over at Rick. "They found a match!"

"A match of what?" Rick asked.

"AFIS matched the prints on the ashtray to those of Marzi!"

"That's great," Rick said. "If this were Boston, we could expect a fairly quick response from the technicians and we'd have him. But we're not in Boston, and Oregon has its big problem of the backup with the OSP examiners."

"I'll call the LT," Patty said. "He may have a suggestion."

Patty explained the AFIS match to the lieutenant, and their predicament with waiting for the fingerprint technician's verification.

"Let me call my contact with OSP," said the lieutenant. "It may be that they can bump up your case now that you have an AFIS match. I'll let you know what I find out. You and Rick on your way back?"

"We are. We pulled over in Garberville to make the call. Should be back in Brookings about eight."

"I'll call you," said the lieutenant, "if I hear anything from OSP before tomorrow morning."

"Thanks, LT. We'll need that piece of the puzzle to put Marzi away, but it doesn't stop us from trying to get a confession out of him with what we've got."

Patty filled Rick in on her conversation with the lieutenant.

"With what we have now," Rick said, "we won't be offering Marzi a deal."

"No deal," Patty said. "Let's see if we can get him to confess with the AFIS match. Of course, his confession won't be necessary once we have the technician's verification, but it might help to convict him for murder rather than involuntary manslaughter. Want me to see if I can set it up for tomorrow afternoon?"

"Anytime after lunch," Rick said.

"I'll set it up for two," Patty said, and made the call.

# CHAPTER 24

At two the next day, Rick and Patty walked into the interview room, where they saw that Marzi was much more nervous than he'd been three days prior. His attorney looked confused. "Why interview my client a second time in three days, Detectives?" he said. "My client's told you everything he knows."

"No," Patty said, "he hasn't." Then, looking at Marzi, Patty asked, "Why'd you break into Lola's house? Was it to kill her and steal her money?"

Marzi sat back in his seat as if he was no longer anxious. "You're asking the same questions you asked the last time we sat together in this room. And like I said then, I didn't kill Lola. Her brother did."

"You made a big mistake, Marzi," Patty said. "When you killed Lola Martin, you left your fingerprints on the green ashtray you used."

Marzi sat stunned as his attorney quickly advised his client not to respond, and the two of them spoke briefly. "Okay," Marzi said. "I was in Lola's house a few times, but only to talk to her. I smoke and probably touched the ashtray when I put out my cigarette."

"Why were you smoking in her bedroom?" Patty asked.

Marzi seemed to go pale. "Like I said, we were just talking. I finished my smoke and noticed the green ashtray sitting there, so I put my cigarette out in it. When I snubbed out my smoke, the ashtray moved and I thought it was going to fall off the table, so I pushed it away from the edge."

Rick took his handcuffs off of his belt and lay them on the table, stacking one cuff onto the other. "Pretend this is the ashtray, Marzi. Show us how you would have moved it away from the edge of the table."

Marzi, now noticeably nervous and shaking, put the tips of his first two fingers up to the edge of the handcuffs and gave them a slight push. "Like that," he said.

"Come on, Marzi," Rick said staring at the man. "We know that's not what happened." Rick then picked up the handcuffs with his right hand, wrapping his fingers around them as though they were a solid object. "We know that you picked up the ashtray like this and hit Lola Martin on the back of the head with it."

Marzi sat stunned and his attorney asked, "Can you prove that, Detective?"

"We sure can," Patti said. "The handprints show the position of the hand and fingers on the ashtray, and their position to the tip of the ashtray that made contact with Lola Martin's head. It clearly shows that Mr. Marzelli's hand was wrapped around the ashtray he used to kill Lola Martin."

Marzi's attorney looked at Rick and Patty and then spoke, again. "Can I have a few minutes with my client?" he asked.

"Sure," Patty said as she and Rick stood up and stepped out of the room.

Five minutes later the attorney opened the door, stuck his head out, and let the detectives know they were ready. Once everyone was seated, he spoke again. "We'll admit to my client accidently killing Lola Martin for a charge of involuntary manslaughter."

"No way." Patty said. "We're charging him with first-degree murder."

"I didn't mean to kill her," Marzi blurted out, now pleading. "I just wanted her money. I thought she was at work and when I entered her bedroom, she screamed at me to leave, and when I didn't she reached up into her closet for her gun on the shelf. I yelled at her that I wasn't there to hurt her. I just wanted the money. 'Just give me the money and I'll leave!' I said. She pulled the gun out of the box and started walking toward me, screaming at me to leave. I didn't know her gun wasn't loaded, and I was afraid she was going to try and kill me. So I shoved her against the wall, picked up the ashtray, and hit her with it. I didn't mean to kill her. I just wanted to stop her so that I could take the money and get out of there."

"When did you know the gun wasn't loaded?" Rick asked

"When I got back to the trailer. I wouldn't have known about it if she hadn't gone to her closet. I just wanted her money."

Patty looked at the man, who now sat bent over with his head lying against his crossed arms on the table. "Why did you clean up the blood and lay Ms. Martin on the bed, Marzi?"

"Because, she was the girl I'd always wanted. I couldn't leave her lying on the floor. I mean, there was so much blood, and it made such a mess. Lola deserved better than that. I looked at her on the bed after I wiped up the blood, and she looked pleased that I'd cleaned up for her."

"Mario Marzelli, you're under arrest for the murder of Lola Martin," Patty said.

Rick and Patty left the room and requested a couple of officers take Marzi back to his cell.

# CHAPTER 25

The next day Patty and Rick were at their desks early, writing up their reports on both the Federal Way surveillance and Marzi's confession. Midmorning they were interrupted with a call over the radio. Someone was attempting to cash a bad check at the local bank. Brad responded to the call. Thirty minutes later he called Patty. "We've got someone in the back of my car who you and Rick might want to talk to before we take him up to Gold Beach."

"Who's that?" Patty asked.

"Jim Severs," Brad said.

"You mean the guy who was playing parking attendant at the Hope Christian Church?"

"One and the same," Brad said. "Seems he took a check out of a purse he snatched from a woman walking down Chetco Avenue, made it payable to himself, walked into the bank, and tried to cash it. You want to talk with him?"

"We sure do," Patty said. "Did you admonish him?"

"Yeah, and he agreed to talk. Said he just found the check."

"Okay," said Patty. "Bring him in to the interview room, and Rick and I will follow."

When Patty completed the call with Brad, she briefed Rick on what was happening. The detectives walked into the room and sat across from Severs, who was handcuffed to the table. "What's your name?" Patty asked.

"Jim Severs," he said.

Patty nodded. "Do you remember the rights Officer Bradley explained to you?"

Jim Severs let out a low laugh. "Of course. I'm no dummy."

Patty and Rick locked eyes, then Patty continued. "Where do you live, Mr. Severs?"

"Right now I'm living in a trailer park off 101."

Patty continued the questioning. "Who asked you to direct parking for attendees at the Hope Christian Church?"

"No one," he said. "I just wanted to make some extra money and the pastor offered to help me out."

"Are you saying that the pastor asked you to play parking attendant?"

"Yeah," Severs said.

"Well, that's not how the pastor tells it. He said that you approached him about directing church attendees where to park. So let's try again. Who asked you to direct parking for the church?"

Severs sat quietly as though thinking about how to answer.

"Let me ask you another way," Patty said. "To whom did you give the attendees' addresses?"

Severs fidgeted in his chair. "I don't know what you're talking about," he said.

"I think you do, Mr. Severs. Are you aware that two of the three burglars you were working with are now in jail, and the third was killed after breaking into a home in Federal Way? The two we have locked up will face murder charges. You'll be charged with murder, too."

"I didn't have anything to do with those murders," Severs said. "I didn't know anyone was going to get hurt. Darren just told me what to do and asked me to get addresses for him. I didn't know anyone was going to get hurt."

Rick handed Severs a pen and yellow tablet. "Write down what happened," Rick said. "Include names and any dates you remember."

"What will you give me if I do this?"

"Only the DA can make a deal," Patty said. "We could talk to the DA and ask him to consider little-to-no jail time for the purse you snatched, and for the check you tried to cash today."

"But you've got to write down everything you told us," Rick said.

After Severs wrote out his activities with the homicide suspects, Patty put him under arrest. "Jim Severs, we're arresting you for murder and theft."

"But you said I might not serve any jail time," Severs said.

"You may not for the purse snatching, but you're going away for a long time for your participation in the murders of two elderly people, and the burglarized homes of several others."

Patty and Rick stepped out of the room to find Brad waiting. "This should tie up the only loose end on those homicides," he said.

Patty smiled. "It does."

*   *   *

Rick looked at his watch. "It's eleven-thirty. Want to go eat?"

"Sure," Patty said. "Got someplace in mind?"

"Well, I'm thinking Wild River Pizza. Sound okay to you?"

"That works," Patty said.

The detectives found a quiet corner table where Rick could see the front door. Rick placed their order and sat down across from Patty. His steel-blue eyes locked into the hazel eyes of his partner. "It's great to have closed both homicide cases. We make a good team, Detective O'Toole."

Patty smiled, "We do at that, Detective Starker." There was silence as they looked at each other, and then Rick spoke. "I'm looking forward to our play date."

Patty rolled her eyes and stood up. "I'll get us a couple plates and napkins."